MW00903721

Bill,

DECEPTION

Enjoy the journey!

JE Gilbert

JE Gilbert

April 2015

PAGE PUBLISHING, INC.
New York, NY

First originally published by Page Publishing, Inc. 2015

ISBN 978-1-62838-936-4 (pbk)
ISBN 978-1-62838-937-1 (digital)
ISBN 978-1-62838-938-8 (hardcover)

Printed in the United States of America

This book is dedicated to my husband Gary, who let me
read out loud to him while I was writing the book
and to my brother Henry, who is my creative thinking partner.

The sun is just beginning to rise. Leslie Turner can see the sky gradually growing lighter. A glance at the digital clock—almost 5:30 a.m., the hour she begins her day. She hopes to greet the morning feeling like herself again. Last night, during dinner and right until she finally fell asleep, she could not shake this nagging, anxious feeling. Leslie closes her eyes again to get whatever sleep she can before her alarm actually goes off.

Little did she know this day would thrust her down a path she may never come back from, testing friendships, her trust in humanity, entering the places her mind did not want to enter. That dark side that demands an inner strength, not something conjured up, but that seed that lies dormant until you need the strength to do the impossible.

Click. The alarm goes off to the sound of "Bad Moon Rising." Although Leslie Turner is only twenty-seven years old, she's gained an appreciation for classic rock. She is by no means a morning person, so waking up to music is a lot better than hearing the drone of the alarm buzz.

Leslie swings her legs over the side of her bed and stands up, all five feet eight inches, and catches her image in the mirror. She pauses a minute to think about what it is that kept her on edge without getting an answer. She studies her long red hair and brown eyes. Eyes that look green in certain lights.

Growing up, her friends would describe her as a pretty girl whose primary focus was school and education. They would agree her life was, at one time, mapped out by her parents, who made it clear they knew what was best. Believing they had everything in place for their daughter, they were shocked when, upon graduating Saint Gerard's High School, Leslie enrolled in the University of Champlain to study interior design.

This did not sit well with her father, the good doctor Henry Turner, MD, or her socialite mother Anne, both well known in the Burlington, Vermont area. Leslie is never one for confrontation especially when it comes to her parents, but her decision to get into interior design came out of pure love for this type of work, and her much-needed ability to breathe, to move in her own direction. Up to that point, she lived a safe, mundane existence, but with the help and support of her best friend Amy Peters, she took a stand to take control of her life and how she was going to live it. To this day, her parents continue to be a bit cool, clearly expressing their feelings of disdain through limited interaction, which one could label as socially acceptable.

It's time to get ready for work; no wasted effort here. By 6:00 a.m., she is ready to go out the door, bed made, pillows and teddy bears back in their proper place. A well-oiled machine with a definite plan on how to attack the day with purpose, and this makes her very happy.

She temporarily forgets the anxious feelings as she steps outside. The day is bright with the littlest hint of fall in the air. She loves this time of year, beginning with September right through the holidays. Leslie starts her car thinking about her best friend Amy. They somehow know when things are going on in each other's life without speaking a word. The nagging, anxious feelings from last night return. Leslie forces them from her mind to think about the day ahead. Her thoughts eventually return to Amy.

She smiles as she thinks about their friendship, which began in the fourth grade at Saint Gerard's Grammar School in Sister Mary

Margaret's class. She laughs out loud as she remembers Sister Margaret, a tough nun who could silently come upon you to squash any fun you may be having inside her classroom, earning her the nickname Space Ghost. Together, Leslie and Amy made that class bearable for each other. Leslie loved Amy. They made a strong connection right from that very first day they met. Amy is bold, takes chances, and goes places Leslie never could. Over the years, Leslie soaked in some of that confidence and the ability to trust in one's self. So it came as no surprise, upon graduating from the University of Champlain, that they would open the Burlington Design Studio. In only four short years, they transformed this folly, as her parents call it, into a well-known, strong business running on all eight cylinders.

Leslie and Amy love Vermont, especially Burlington, located on the eastern shore of Lake Champlain. The area is simply captivating and surrounded by scenic beauty. Their studio is not far from Church Street. It's a great location with lots of foot traffic. People are drawn to them. Amy is the tall one, almost six feet, with short curly black hair and blue eyes; eyes that sparkle with mischief. Amy is unaware of how much she contributes to their success by simply being herself.

As her car rolls into the parking lot, her pulse increases and she feels herself smile. The satisfaction she feels is sinful. Leslie parks to the far right of the parking lot because she loves to walk past the display window and examine it as if she were a potential customer. Her eyes take in the display, looking to see if there is something to entice her to go inside. Her brisk movements now slow to a crawl. Taking small steps, absorbing all she sees, she analyzes the layout, stops, and placing her hand on the side of her face, postures a yes movement with her head. She hears herself say, "I must go inside; these girls are good."

Key in hand, she unlocks the front door going through it in a flash, laughing at herself and hoping no one is watching her. Her first task is to get the coffee brewing. She is in the process of checking the answering machine when Amy enters. "What's up, Red?" Red is a name Leslie is not fond of but one that Amy uses to tease her. She thinks it helps lighten Leslie's more serious side. Leslie ignores her. "The Darringtons would like to see one of us to discuss what we can do with, according to Mrs. Darrington, their drab house." Amy already decided Leslie is the right person for this job. Mrs. Darrington is a bit of a talker, and she will take hours to make up her mind. As Leslie looks toward her best friend and business partner, she can see her shaking her head. "It will have to be you, Red. I'm finishing up on our proposal for that medical center down in Portland. But I need coffee first." Amy starts to move in the direction of the small kitchen in search of that coffee when she's prevented from making any headway. Leslie leads her into the office and motions to a chair for her to sit down. "Amy, the coffee is brewing and we need to talk."

Amy gives Leslie the best concerned look she can muster. "About what?" Leslie smiles at her as she breaches the topic she is unsure will go over very well.

"You know we need another full-time employee and at least one, possibly two, part-time people." The words rush out fast, and Leslie holds her breath, waiting for Amy's response. Amy leans forward, and looking Leslie square in the eyes, replies, "I agree." And with that declaration, she springs from her seat to retrieve that much-needed cup of coffee.

"That's it?" Leslie calls after her. Amy always amazes Leslie with her decision-making. It's quick and right on the money; after all, Amy came up with the joint venture concept for the Burlington Design Studio. Leslie smiles. Another wonderfully busy day gets underway and, like many others, progresses much faster than either of them can anticipate. There is never a shortage of things to do.

"Amy, it's four o'clock. I'm heading up to the Darringtons'. I'm not sure how long this meeting will take, so can you close up?"

Amy calls out, "Will do, and by the way, how is your boyfriend?" This question is on the same level as calling Leslie Red. Amy sits back in her chair and waits for her friends' reaction. "What boyfriend?" Leslie responds as she gathers her samples and design ideas for the meeting with the Darrington's.

"Oh, come on, Leslie. You know, Alexander! You have known him for four years now."

"We're just friends." replies Leslie.

"A man doesn't hang around for four years just to be friends. Although, you know how your life seems to unfold in four year increments."

This comment halts her gathering process confusing her at exactly what her friend is suggesting. "Where are you going with this, Amy?" Amy enters her office and, using her fingers, counts off. "High school, four years; college, four years; this establishment, four years; and he is present at the beginning, may I remind you." Leslie knows Amy means well but she never makes quick decisions, especially when it comes to the heart.

"I know, but I need our business to make it and not just survive. Make it to a scale that will impress, you know?"

"You better move, Red, or you just might lose Alexander, and then you won't have to worry about it." With this said, Amy turns on her heels and walks out, returning to work on the proposal.

"Amy, I've got to go. I'm running late," Leslie says, walking toward the front door, her arms filled with samples and design ideas. It's a short drive across town to the Darrington's colonial home. She focuses her mind on their meeting and pushes the conversation with Amy out.

Leslie's meeting with the Darrington's goes well. Almost three hours well. Leslie is worried about their ability to complete the work before they hire more help, if they even get this job. As she drives toward home, she decides to stop by the studio to pick up a few additional samples she wants to show the Darrington's in the morning. Her plan is to make them her first stop. She is keenly aware that the anxious feeling she felt last night and again this morning has returned. She tries to explain it away as coming from the amount of work they have versus their number of employees.

It is nearly 7:30 p.m. when Leslie pulls into the parking lot, and the lights are still on inside the studio. "Amy must be working late," Leslie says aloud. As she comes through the front door, she calls out, "Hello," but there is no answer, just the shop stereo playing in the background. Leslie heads for the back room; and there behind the counter is Amy's baseball bat, the persuader as she calls it, lying on the floor. Then it hit her, that chill that tells you something bad has happened. She is sure the anxiety she felt last night and earlier today is connected to this moment. She is frozen in midstride, fearful, her heart pounding loudly in her chest, drowning out her ability to hear any other sounds. She's afraid to see what awaits her in the back room, and she chastises herself for letting her imagination get the best of her.

"Amy…Amy are you here?" She knows she has to go in the back room and is hoping Amy just ran out to the deli for something. With legs moving again, she enters and stops dead in her tracks. There on the floor is Amy, blood dripping from the wounds on her head, pooling on the wood floor. Leslie cannot move. She instinctively grabs the telephone to dial 911.

Only a few seconds transpire, but Leslie feels like she is frozen in time in a place that should feel more familiar than it does at this moment. She's unsure how long she's been standing there when she hears the front door open. The first to arrive on the scene is Sergeant Harold Youngblood. He sees her anguished expression, the loss of color from her face, and the way she's standing perfectly still, making him realize he has to do something quick.

Leslie is numb, staring toward the back room. Youngblood walks over to stand in front of her. Leslie takes in this ruggedly handsome guy who looks much younger than what is most likely his forty years. He is six feet five inches tall, and she can tell he prides himself on staying in shape.

"I'm Sergeant Harold Youngblood," he says as he holds up his badge in front of her. "What is your name? Your name dear…" From somewhere far away, she hears herself respond, "My name is Leslie." Youngblood recognizes her as Leslie Turner, the daughter of Henry and Anne Turner. Gently touching her arm he asks, "Did you call this in?"

"Yes…yes…back there…" Leslie nods toward the back of the studio, and in that instant, her attention is once again gone, lost in whatever he has yet to see for himself in the back room.

Youngblood quickly surveys the studio, and placing his hands on Leslie's arms, he guides her to the storefront and sits her down in an enormous wing chair. Leslie looks up at him still in a trance but feeling grateful to have distance between her and the back room. She tries to make some sense out of what is going on. "Did you touch anything, Leslie?" he asks her. "No," she replies, and in that moment, Leslie is bothered by her lack of action upon discovering Amy's body in spite of how close the two of them are. She just couldn't force herself to touch her.

Youngblood can see her focus is once again lost. He squats down in front of her and breaks the silence saying, "Leslie…Leslie, stay here. I'm going to look around." Youngblood makes his way to the back room. There on the floor, he finds Amy Peters. Youngblood's first job is to check the girl's body, being very careful not to disturb anything. He touches her wrist; she is still warm to the touch but has no pulse. He figures this happened within the past few hours. It didn't look like a rape occurred; his eyes move around the studio, taking in as much of the crime scene as possible. He pauses, looking at the counter where the baseball bat lay on the floor; and there on the lower shelf is a cash box, open, standing on end as if it were thrown. He'll ask Leslie about how much money the box held at a later time.

Over his fifteen years on the force, he'd seen many victims and colleagues suffer from seeing tragedy, causing them to embrace many different solutions to cope. He chose exercise and staying in shape. Youngblood gazes back at Leslie; he didn't need to call upon his experience to realize she is going to need support through this, but he also knew very little would come from talking with her today.

Youngblood hears the sirens as the officers arrive along with the crime scene technicians. He gives them clearance to begin working the crime scene. Youngblood is going to escort Leslie home. It is a good plan plus he wants to get her out of here before a certain detective arrives.

2

"Where the hell do you think you're going with her?" Youngblood did not have to look back to recognize the voice as belonging to Detective Charles Upton, a Neanderthal among men. Youngblood felt regret. If only he moved a little quicker or the Neanderthal a little slower. He wondered how a man with such a large head could house a brain so small. He mused, perhaps this is where the phrase "fathead" originated. Youngblood did not halt his forward motion; he merely slowed down to call out, "I'm taking her home. We can talk with her tomorrow." He continues moving forward, keeping the sight of his Jeep Cherokee patrol car as their destination.

Detective Charles Upton is fifty-six years old, five foot five and three-hundred-plus pounds. His suits always appear rumpled and his comb-over slick. Upton has been on the force for twenty-five years, a fact that brings him extreme pleasure when dealing with Youngblood. He wasn't well liked. Round like a barrel, the men referred to him behind his back as "bottom of the barrel."

"I'm the head detective here, Youngblood. I'm the man in charge."

"No argument there" and in a softer voice adds, "You are the number one dickhead."

Youngblood continues leading Leslie toward the front door never breaking his stride. "WHAT?" Upton blasts. It seemed impossible to everyone that Upton could speak any louder, but somehow he could muster a tone that sent animals running and caused all foot traffic to come to a stop. Youngblood handed Leslie off to one of the patrol cops and turned back to meet Upton face-to-face as he stormed toward him.

"You are in charge, Charles, but do you know who that is?"

"Just some broad—some scared broad—and also my best lead."

Youngblood always did his homework to know as many of the town's citizens as he possibly could. He reads the paper faithfully looking at each section, Leisure, Gossip, Sports, and any portion that could keep him informed about what is going on in Burlington. Youngblood also gets online at least once daily. Lowering his voice and standing close to Upton he tells him, "She is not just any broad, Charles." Their close proximity works just as Youngblood hoped, and Upton turns down his volume, "Then who the fuck is she? Sister Theresa?"

"No, that is Leslie Turner." Upton looks over at Leslie and takes in the attractive woman with long red hair.

"Is that the bitch that dances over at the Jungle Room? Ya think she'll honor us with a little number now? She can use my pole." Youngblood is tempted to lay Upton out. He's speechless with fists clenched. He knows if he is going to get this encounter under control he has to be calm.

"Think, Upton. Did you ever hear the names, Mr. and Mrs. Henry and Anne Turner?" Thinking he's smart and seizing the opportunity to get the better of Youngblood, Upton replies, "Do they dance there too?" Youngblood can't believe this man made the detective grade. He could only rationalize this by believing Upton was promoted before there was too much crime and when life was a lot simpler. "No, Charles. The Turners know the captain; they are active members of the Vermont Police Association and no strangers to contributing both time and money to the work we do. I dare think that bullet proof vest you're donning was contributed by them."

"Okay…okay, but she ain't goin' anywhere until I say that she can."

"Again, I'm urging you to think, Upton. Her parents have a lot of pull; they know the right people, and they are very active in our community. Plus Leslie is in shock. We're not going to get anything from her tonight that can't wait"

Losing his patience and feeling confused about what exactly is his point, Upton's frustration comes through loud and clear, "Okay... okay. So what are you saying?"

"Do you want to stay a detective?"

Upton turns to walk away from Youngblood and, without hesitating, replies, "This letting her leave is on you, Youngblood. Go drop her off and hurry back. Oh, and don't be sampling anything along the way."

Upton never ceases to amaze Youngblood. It is hard to believe that he continues to act the way he does. He can singlehandedly set them back twenty years. How is it possible that he keeps his job? Youngblood walks over to get Leslie, and as they are leaving, Alexander Acof is heading toward the studio.

Alexander comes by the studio at least once a day. He likes to come for two reasons. One, Leslie and Amy hired him to remodel their shop, and he enjoys looking over what he feels is his best carpentry work. And two, he likes to see Leslie and spend some time with her. He loves being near her, and he knows she is his girl and he is her guy even though it is unspoken. Leslie just hasn't realized this yet.

As Alexander approaches, his steps quicken and his heart is starting to pound. He's concerned over the large scale police presence and their movement around the Burlington Design Studio. At twenty-seven, Alexander is strong from working hard at his family's construction business. He stands six feet four inches tall with short hair. He's clean shaven and weighs two hundred and forty pounds, and it's all muscle.

Without hesitation, he pushes past the patrolman at the door only to run smack into Detective Upton.

"Stop right there." Upton places his hand on Alexander's chest, somehow stopping his forward movement.

"Is Leslie all right?"

"And just who might you be?" Upton takes in Alexander from head to toe.

"I'm Alexander Acof," he replies, looking over Upton's head hoping desperately to process all the police activity.

"Just what is your concern here?"

"I'm Leslie's boyfriend; is she all right?" Alexander is frantic.

"Leslie is just fine. Officer Harold Youngblood just left to drive her home, but the other girl isn't."

Alexander takes a half step back, feeling like the wind is knocked out of him.

"Amy?"

"Before we go any further I want to see your license or some sort of ID." Alexander hands over his license and Upton checks it out. A half smirk comes over his face, and he yells to the patrolman posted on the front door, "Bob, sit Alexander here in your patrol car and guard him until I can get to him." Alexander lets Bob lead him to his patrol car.

"Is Amy dead?"

"Yes."

"How did it happen?"

Bob knows better than to answer any more questions, and he silently holds the door to his patrol car open for Alexander to climb in. Upton yells, "And this time, try not to let him push his way past you again!"

It took about one hour for Upton to finish his investigative assessment when Youngblood returns. On his way into the Burlington Design Studio, Youngblood spies Acof in the patrol car. He sees Alexander place his cell phone to his ear.

Alexander's head is still spinning with a million unanswered questions. He can't wait to get out of this patrol car. Then he realizes his cell phone is inside his jacket. He pushes the speed dial number assigned to Leslie. Her voice sounds foreign as she answers her cell phone. "Leslie, are you all right?"

"Yes, Alexander, I think so. Where are you?"

"I'm outside the studio. They told me Amy is dead."

"I can't think straight, and I can't talk about it. I keep replaying what I saw. I called my mom and dad, and they should be here any minute to get me. I can't be alone tonight." This makes Alexander feel somewhat better.

"If you need me, Leslie, call my cell phone. It doesn't matter what time." Leslie feels a rush of gratitude.

"Love you, Al. I'll call you tomorrow."

Youngblood approaches Upton, who is barking out last minute commands to the forensic team. "Why do you have someone in that patrol car?" Youngblood asks, knowing full well it's Alexander Acof.

"For your information, he can be the killer returning to the scene of the crime." Youngblood knows Upton doesn't believe this.

"If that's what you think then why isn't he handcuffed and why would you let him use his cell phone?" Upton is going to lose it. His voice booms as he points to the patrol car, "Bob, get that goddamn cell phone away from him, now!" Youngblood had never officially met Alexander Acof, but he's seen him around town and is familiar with his work. A carpenter by trade, working for his father, the owner of the Acof Construction Company. There are many occasions when he's driving an Acof Construction pickup truck around town. Youngblood needs to know what he's missing that led to detaining him.

"Upton, what do you know?"

"This is quick, easy, and simple. It's a drug-related incident. Anyone can see that. It's obvious."

"So what are you saying, Detective? You think this kid is the murderer, and it's driven by drugs? And he decided to return to the scene of the crime with police present?"

Upton pauses for a second. "No, I don't. I just didn't like the way he came pushing his way in and asking a lot of questions."

Youngblood continues to press, "Okay, go on…"

"It looks like the cash box was emptied and the victim tried to stop the perp, and he overpowered her. It does not appear anything else was touched. We canvassed all the neighbors, but no one saw or heard anything. I had the body moved to the morgue, and as far as I'm concerned, I'm releasing the crime scene."

Youngblood shook his head, feeling a bit exasperated. "So you put Alexander Acof in the patrol car?"

"Yes, I did and while we're on this topic how the hell do you know his name may I ask? Are you the great Carnac?"

"I recognized the kid on my way in, plus Leslie filled me in on a few facts regarding who is a regular visitor during her workday. Tonight, she's staying with her parents. She'll speak with us tomorrow at the precinct by 10:00 a.m."

"You know, Youngblood, you continue to be a real pain in my ass."

3

Alexander just finished cleaning up his tools when his cell phone rings. He is happy to read Leslie's name on the display screen. It is 2:00 p.m. and this is their first conversation since last night, and for the first time, he feels relieved. "Hello, Leslie. Are you okay?"

With a big exhaled sigh, Leslie replies, "I'm doing okay. I just finished with the police. I'll be at the studio after 3:00 p.m. Detective Upton told me they will release the studio as a crime scene by then, and I'm free to go back there after that. I'm so mixed up, Al. I don't understand anything that's happened. Amy is dead."

"Is there anything I can do?" Leslie didn't need anything. "No, I just want to see you, Al. Maybe you can help me make some sense out of what happened. As far as the studio goes, thank goodness for Kathleen because she's taking care of calling all our pressing appointments and rescheduling the rest. She's holding down the fort from home and will meet me at the studio." Alexander is happy to hear Kathleen is helping her keep things running as normally as possible.

"I have a few things to take care of and then I'll meet you as soon as I finish."

"Okay. I'll see you later. I'm going to check on Amy's parents and find out if I can help with the arrangements once the body is released from the morgue."

Alexander feels strange driving up to the studio. One of the people he enjoys seeing won't be there to welcome him at the door and tease him. He can only imagine what it must feel like for Leslie.

As he enters, he spots Leslie sitting in the large wing chair at the front of the studio, legs up to her chest, arms hugging her legs with her chin resting on her knees. She is staring straight ahead looking like a little girl. He wishes he could make all her pain disappear.

Alexander walks over and squats in front of Leslie. "Are you all right?" He waits a beat, and when she does not reply, he offers, "Leslie, I wish I knew what to do or say to bring you comfort, but this kind of loss is never easy." Leslie looks into the face of Alexander. He is a strong man and a great friend. "I appreciate you. Al. I can't think of anything that can make me feel better. I wish I could but short of going back in time and changing this horrible outcome…" She shakes her head and her eyes fill with tears. "I don't think I can do this any longer. I don't have what it takes. We were a great team."

Alexander gives Leslie some tough love. "You are not alone. If you need someone, use me. If you need a reason to do this work, do it for Amy." Her anger flares. In one swift movement, she has both feet on the floor, arms on the armrests; her eyes lasers on Alexander with one goal in mind, to set the record straight.

Before she can say a word, the studio door opens and in walks Sergeant Youngblood. His eyes take in both Leslie and Alexander. He can cut the tension with a knife. "I was in the vicinity. I thought I would check in on you to make sure you were okay. Hello, Alexander." Alexander nods his head. He's grateful for the interruption.

With a heavy sigh Leslie looks at Youngblood and replies, "I'm fine, I guess, Sergeant Youngblood. I don't even know. Have you heard anything?"

"No, not much, I'm afraid. Detective Upton believes he has everything tied up. Although there is one thing, it seems someone slipped into the jewelry store that night a few shops down on the opposite corner and took a small display case off the countertop. It had about forty pairs of earrings valued from eighty to one hundred forty dollars each." Leslie's first reaction is disbelief.

"Whenever Mr. Allison leaves their jewelry store, his daughter Dorothy activates the motion sensor by flipping a switch in the back room. It looks like that's when the perp slipped in and grabbed the case. Dorothy heard the sensor go off as she reentered the storefront, and her attention was drawn to the closing door. From the corner of her eye, she caught movement as the perp went around the corner of the building. The timing is consistent with what happened here."

Alexander broke in, asking Youngblood, "Did she go after the person?"

"No, she had no reason to at that time. She didn't realize anything was missing until this morning. The excitement of the police activity most likely added to the discovery being delayed."

Leslie is confused. "If it is a random robbery, what does it have to do with what happened here? This was murder." She begins to cry again, turning her head away.

Youngblood wants to continue the conversation but is hesitant to keep going. Leslie looks back at him, and he can see she wants him to go on. "We think the perp knew what to take and when to do it. You see, the Allison's never put the sensor on during the day because of the volume of foot traffic. When only one person is in their shop, they turn it on. That leads us to believe our perp knew this. If he knew this, he was most likely watching them and also the two of you."

Leslie felt a chill go through her as she thought about his words and involuntarily pulled her legs back up into her chest and hugged them. Alexander could tell she is frightened. He shook his head.

"You are not reassuring us Sergeant Youngblood." Youngblood looks at them.

"I know, but it's better to be safe. You may have even seen this person."

Leslie said out loud, trancelike, "They were watching us?"

"I wouldn't doubt it, Leslie. Maybe you should consider getting a door sensor. Video seems to be a good deterrent."

Leslie felt a flash of anger. She could not find the value in doing this now. After all, she lost someone very precious to her, and she is not sure she even wants to keep the business. "I think it is a bit too late for that, don't you? Everything has changed."

Youngblood understood; it's her grief talking. He sees terrible things happen on such a regular basis that maybe his perspective is gone. But he is thinking she still had her whole life in front of her, and giving up on something she obviously loves is not a good option. "It's never too late when this work is something you love and you're good at it. People in this area are saddened about what happened to you, and we are going to figure out who did this. There have been a lot of robberies that are drug related. These people have more nerve that you can ever imagine. Quite often they will return."

Alexander is quiet then asks Youngblood, "Are you saying this was drug related?" Youngblood shrugs his shoulder.

"Can't rule it out yet. You see, when it comes to robbing a series of stores, it is not unusual to choose the places located at the ends. It gives them the advantage of getting in and out quickly. It limits their need to pass in front of another store, which would increase their chance of being seen by someone." Leslie stood.

"Where was this information when we rented this location?"

Youngblood recognized it's time to move on. His training taught him well. "Leslie, if you should need me or if you remember something, even the smallest detail, call me. Here is my card with my cell phone number on the back." Leslie liked Youngblood, and although she was told to contact Detective Upton, she didn't want to.

"I don't know if I can. I was told to call Detective Upton, but quite honestly, he frightens me."

"I will stay in touch and you can feel safe calling me." With that, Youngblood is at the door, doorknob in hand when he turns to look at Leslie. "Trust me, Leslie, he frightens me too." Not waiting for a response, he is out of the studio, headed in the direction of the Allison's jewelry store.

Leslie is silently thinking about their conversation with Youngblood. The studio is a bit quiet; the stereo wasn't playing, and the primary background noise is the ticking of their grandfather clock. Leslie asks Alexander, "How does Youngblood know you?"

"I never met him until last night, but I've seen him around town.

I remember people. Cops do the same; they remember people, and somehow they get to know if someone belongs here or not. In our town, people come from all over to visit. Having someone who is good at that is a real asset."

Alexander takes Leslie by the hand. He wants to get her out of the studio for a while, thinking they had enough discussion about what happened for today. "Since Kathleen is here and has everything under control, how about we go get something to eat? I bet you haven't eaten today."

"I haven't but…"

Alexander shrugs his shoulders. "You have to eat sometime, and after we eat, I'd like you to meet this friend of mine."

"Really, Alexander, why would I want to meet this friend of yours today? What would be the purpose?"

Alexander takes her into his confidence. "My friends name is John, and he owns a pawnshop. He sometimes hears and learns about certain things the police don't."

"Are you thinking he may know something about what happened here, Al?"

"No, not exactly. I'm thinking more along the lines of what happened at the jewelry store. If this is drug related, the perp needs to turn the stolen goods around. Most likely into cash, and a pawnshop is the best place to do this. If these two incidents are linked, we can get a heads up on just who this person is."

"Al, tell me how you know John and don't tell me it's because you've seen him around town."

Alexander settles back into his chair, preparing to share more detail with Leslie to earn her trust. She can be so innocent at times and so smart at others. This made him want to protect her even more. "John is more of a friend of my Dad. You see, tools disappear all the time, especially on a big job site. For example, at John's, we can pick up a Hitachi nail gun. A new one runs six hundred to nine hundred dollars. At the pawnshop, we can pick it up for one hundred to three hundred dollars."

"Did you ever think you might be buying back your own tools?"

"Sometimes. But when we buy a tool, we paint it green, red, and yellow so it helps us identify what's ours on the job site when we're securing everything at the end of the workday."

Leslie chuckled. "Can't say I care for your color code."

Alexander smiles at her. "It makes it harder for someone to walk off with something, and John lets us know if anything turns up at his shop."

"So what you're saying is John is honorable."

Alexander purses his lips and nods. "Not exactly. He and my dad have some kind of arrangement worked out. If the pawnshop receives something questionable, John puts it in the back room for a certain period of time, or it can be shipped off to a specific location."

Leslie is too exhausted and feels uncomfortable going to a pawnshop. "Al, I've never been to a pawnshop, and I'm not feeling inclined to go to one tonight."

"All pawnbrokers are not dishonest. This business is known to draw a certain element there at times."

"So let me get this straight, construction and drugs go hand in hand."

"No. Drugs can happen to anyone. We had a roofer who was good at his trade, but he was also a notorious drug user. All his money went to booze and drugs. He had no home; in fact, we have some workers who live in their vans on the job site."

Leslie grappled with this new information. It is just too much to process. She is definitely missing his point. She needs to speak to someone. "Al, this is just too much for me today. I'll go with you to meet John, but it will have to be tomorrow. I really need to talk with someone."

"I'm here… listening."

"I need to talk to a priest I know. Too much has happened. I need someone who isn't tied so closely to this in any way. Can you understand that?" Alexander did understand.

"I'll be here to get you tomorrow about 4:00 p.m."

Leslie gives him a hug and picks up the phone to order deli sandwiches to be delivered for her and Kathleen. After what happened, no one will ever be in the studio alone again especially after their 7:00 p.m. closing time.

4

On her drive over to Saint Gerard's, an uneasy feeling builds inside Leslie as she looks around. She remembers this area from her childhood as very pristine. Everywhere she looks, there are street and homeless people. There are abandoned cars, and the once tidy streets are now scattered with garbage. At another point in time, she feels confident she wouldn't respond this way, but not tonight, not now. It seems funny to Leslie that she never saw any of this on her weekly drive over here to attend church, or maybe she is seeing the world differently now.

As she pulls up to a stoplight, she can see Saint Gerard's with its church towering over the other buildings. It held many fond childhood memories; the name Amy and their first Holy Communion, Confirmation, Easter Sunday, Christmas Midnight Mass, and much more.

As a smile starts to form on her lips, Leslie is slammed back into reality when a homeless man invades her view to clean the windshield. She did not see him coming, or she would have discouraged him long before he had the opportunity to get started. Putting her side window down about one inch, she speaks to him in her best calm voice she can muster since she does not want to upset him, "No thank you. That's not necessary."

Unfortunately, the homeless man is applying the second application of his secret concoction. Instinctively, she pulls her purse closer while she keeps her eyes on him. Youngblood had given her pepper spray; not just any pepper spray, but police issue. Just having her hand on it makes her feel better.

This man is unshaven, filthy, his clothes stained everywhere. The hair on his head is matted and has not seen a comb or a brush in a very long time. He has a most perfectly proportioned gray streak down the center of his head from his forehead to his back.

As the squeegee pulls across the windshield one last time, he peers into the window. Leslie, no longer feeling terrified, releases the pepper spray and pulls out the change from the deli delivery. The smallest denomination is a five dollar bill. Rolling it up, she puts it through the open window. He grabs the bill, and when he realizes its denomination, yells, "Thank you, sweetie!" She gets a good view of his yellow teeth with food trapped between them.

Leslie hits the gas without caring whether or not the light turned green. She looks in her rearview mirror and sees his squeegee, which must have gotten hooked on her car, launch into the air and crash to the ground like a dysfunctional firework rocket. He watches in horror as his most precious work tool is yanked from his hand. "Hey!" is all she hears him yell.

Her focus is putting distance between them and she obsesses about how badly her car now needs to be washed. Moving fast, she barely makes the turn into the parking lot of Saint Gerard's, screeching into a parking space. She turns off the car and sits there for a minute or two, getting her breathing under control.

She enters the side entrance of the rectory so the homeless man cannot see her. Leslie used this entrance many times while attending school at Saint Gerard's. Inside the entryway, there are stairs down to the basement and up to the kitchen where Mrs. O'Brien, the housekeeper, is usually found. She hears her familiar humming.

Mrs. O'Brien is pleasantly surprised to see Leslie Turner. "Well, hello, Leslie! It's been a long time!"

Leslie rushes into her open arms. "Mrs. O'Brien, you have not changed one bit!"

The hug feels good and brings back old times. Mrs. O'Brien attended the morning's church Mass for Amy, but they didn't have a chance to talk. "I'm sorry about Amy. It's tragic." Leslie nods her agreement.

"What can I do for you, dear?" Leslie tells her she wants to speak with Father Figuora, and Mrs. O'Brien leads her down the hall to his office. Upon entering, Leslie can see he is not there at the moment. "Make yourself at home, dear, while I go get father for you."

Father Figuora's office is located in the front of the rectory. The furniture is made of beautiful, ornate dark, rich wood. Leslie knew how much Alexander would appreciate its quality. She walks to the front window to look out on Main Street. From where she stands, she can see the homeless man she encountered not five minutes earlier.

"Leslie!" Never hearing Father Figuora approach, she is startled.

"Hello, father. I need to talk with you."

"Sure, Leslie, please sit wherever you like." He motions with his hand around the room, offering up many seating options, but Leslie's attention returns to looking out the window. Father Figuora comes up behind her to see what she's looking at. "What do you see, sweetie?"

"When did this area fall into such disrepair? It was such a beautiful place five years ago. It seems like the homeless people have taken over?"

Father Figuora looks in the direction she faces. He catches sight of the homeless man. "Oh, you mean Skunk?" Leslie turns to look at him.

"The man on the corner is named Skunk?" Father Figuora smiles at her.

"Yes. I imagine it's his hair that prompted that nickname. He's a good man who's fallen on some hard times. I have him do odd jobs for me from time to time." He touches her on the arm and sweeps the room with his other hand, prompting her to take a seat.

Leslie's first thought is he might be called Skunk for other reasons. She is distracted by the fact Father Figuora called her sweetie. That is just weird, especially from a priest. In that moment, she realizes she's lost all her interest in talking with him. Now all she can think about is getting out of there.

He leads her over to a small grouping of furniture, and they sit down. "Leslie, how can I help you?"

"I'm sorry, father. I thought I was ready to talk about Amy, but now I realize I'm not. It feels too soon."

Father Figuora sits back, studying Leslie. "You know, dear, God has a plan…"

She cuts him off before he can go any further. She just does not want a sermon right now. "No, father, I realize now it's still too raw. I can't talk about Amy yet. I promise I'll come back when I'm ready."

Father Figuora stands with her. "I'll be here when you're ready." He walks Leslie toward the front door, but she stops.

"I'd like to go out through the kitchen, father; this way I can say good-bye to Mrs. O'Brien."

"Okay, dear. You just go ahead, and I hope to see you soon."

With that, Father Figuora returns to his office and closes the door. Walking down the hall, Leslie continues to admire the woodworking built by a craftsman. Crown molding with detailed trim. She smiles at the thought of Alexander's influence.

Entering the kitchen brings a big smile back to Mrs. O'Brien's face. She wipes her hands on her apron and looks at Leslie.

"Mrs. O'Brien, I never did thank you for how you always treated me and Amy so well."

"Oh my dear, you made it so easy. Do you have time for a cup of tea?"

"Yes, I most certainly do." Mrs. O'Brien went into motion. She had a kettle already brewing with plenty of hot water for both of them. She set the table in a flash, added a few of her homemade cookies, and in no time at all, they are seated facing each other.

"Mrs. O'Brien, when did things get so bad and run down around here? It's only been about five years since I was here on a regular basis, and it seems so different," Leslie said.

"It looks worse than it actually is. It's not so bad down here." She smiles at Leslie. Maybe her reaction to the area is just blown out of proportion because of what happened two days earlier, but what she really wants is to know more about the man they call Skunk.

"That man outside that they call Skunk…"

"Oh him. He comes in here a lot, and I'm unsure really why."

"He does?" Mrs. O'Brien nods her head yes and rolls her eyes.

"He's with father quite often. Maybe he's trying to get him back on the right path."

"Yes, father mentioned he uses him for odd jobs?"

Mrs. O'Brien shrugged, "Father uses a lot of people; in fact, three of our best football players, Brad Preston, Leon Banks, and Bernard Genetti are always hanging around here or with father." They sipped their tea and fell quiet for a minute or two.

"What does he use the football players for?"

"I really don't know, but I'll tell you one thing, those boys are too high-strung for me."

Their conversation and tea is finished, and it's time to take her leave. She thanks Mrs. O'Brien. It felt good to see her again, and she promises to not be a stranger. Compared to the way she felt upon arriving, she left with a warm, familiar, comforting feeling.

5

The alarm goes off, and Leslie lay there. She isn't really sleeping. She had to get to work. People depended on her. She took a minute to thank God for Mrs. O'Brien who helped her feel better yesterday. She jumps up; it is time to get it in gear. It's only a matter of time before Leslie is in the studio, and Kathleen comes strolling in.

"Good morning, Ms. Turner. Shall I start the coffee?" Kathleen asks. "Thanks for asking, Kathleen. It's on, and do me a favor, call me Leslie." Her mind drifts to how much she'd love to hear her best friend call her Red right now.

Kathleen is a divorced single mother. Leslie wants to give her more responsibilities, but she's unsure of what toll the extra demands will make on her home life. "Kathleen, I'm either going to hire another full time employee, or I'm thinking of moving Russell to full time. What makes more sense?" Kathleen is flattered Leslie included her. Her first reaction is to ask, "Do we have other options?"

"Yes, in fact, there are design students from the college who always look for this type of work. Maybe that's an option." Kathleen stood, moving her weight from one foot to the other.

"Kathleen, I need you. We think alike, and I'd like to put more of the daily business details on you. I'd also give you a raise; it may not be really big because I'm thinking you and your daughter could use benefits first." Kathleen barely contains her excitement.

"I'm…I'm…YES, I can handle it! Thank you Leslie!" Leslie is thrilled. "I don't believe Russell wants more hours or responsibility. It's probably best to think about a design student. Would I train this person?"

Leslie agrees. "Yes, I think that would be best. Are we good?"

"As far as I'm concerned." With that, Kathleen gets to work.

The day moves along very fast, which is good as far as Leslie is concerned. It's good to be occupied. When she did look up, it is almost 5:00 p.m.; and just as she wonders where Alexander is, he walks through the front door.

Alexander smiles and announces, "Dinnertime."

"Hey, I thought you were going to be here by four? Is everything okay?"

"Yes, I got tied up, and I still need to run over to Saint Albans to pick something up. Come with me."

Leslie turns to Kathleen. "I'm leaving now Kathleen. Isn't Russell coming in?"

"Yes. He will be here any minute."

Alexander takes her arm, and they walk out the front door to where he parked his pickup truck. He holds the door as she climbs in. Leslie puts on her seatbelt and looks around his truck. She could not help thinking what a real guy Alexander is.

"You know, Al, you can wash this truck once in a while or at least clean the windows." Alexander chuckles.

"You sound just like my dad. He wants every vehicle in his fleet looking shiny and new. He says it speaks well for his construction company. Well, let's get out of here and get something to eat. I'm starving." Leslie puts her hand on his arm and squeezes it.

"Just hold on a minute or two."

"But I'm hungry," Alexander whines.

"Just wait." He can feel her body relax once she sees Russell pull into the studio's parking lot. She releases his arm, letting him know they can leave.

They drive in comfortable silence, unwinding from a hectic day's work and feeling good to be in each other's company. It is nice to know conversation is unnecessary. Alexander pulls up in front of a small Italian restaurant in Saint Albans. Leslie is pleasantly surprised.

"Al, I thought dinner for you construction types is Burger King or Arby's?" Al laughs.

"We can go to either place if you prefer. But me, personally, I like to eat here whenever I'm over this way. It doesn't boast a fine wine list and there are no tablecloths, but the food is out of this world."

They sit at a small table in the front window. The restaurant lighting is dark with small white twinkling lights that set the atmosphere. The waitress comes over to take their order. Alexander orders his favorite dish, chicken parmesan while Leslie's choice is meat ravioli. Alexander knew Leslie would love this place.

"Alexander, you really enjoy your work don't you?"

He nods yes. "I believe without work you're lost. Work gives you a reason for your existence, a purpose, and if it challenges you, satisfaction and pride. It helps complete you and gives you an outline."

She thought they were a lot alike, but now she's sure. She feels the same way; although working without Amy will be challenging, she knows she can't give up the studio. It is her life. Alexander reads her thoughts. "We're a lot alike, Red."

She feels herself blush. There was a time when hearing someone call her Red was like nails on the chalkboard, but in that moment, she appreciated this nickname. Dinner is great just as Alexander predicted. As they drive back toward Burlington, Leslie is curious where the pawnshop is located.

"His shop is located where you won't find fine wines and designer clothes." He smiles.

"I'm beginning to think you and your dad know some really interesting people."

Alexander thought, if you only knew. "My dad is a good man. Remember, he came out of Russia fifteen years ago when Russia was falling apart, and you needed to know certain people to survive."

Leslie interjects, "Like John the pawnbroker?"

"Yes, just like that. There is more to him than meets the eye. Well, here we are."

The buildings in this part of town are all brick. This area had seen better times but the brick architecture was ornate. Most of the buildings are closed businesses except for a liquor store and John's pawnshop.

Alexander looks at her and says, "Let me do the talking." Leslie had no plans on talking but did offer something said under her breath, "They don't believe in clean windows over here either."

As they enter the pawnshop, Leslie sees everything imaginable. There are even some bolts of material on a table next to an armoire and the most beautiful china cabinet she has ever seen. John's face lights up when he sees Alexander, "Well, hell-o, Alexander," he greeted and he holds out his hand for a handshake.

Alexander smiles broadly. "Hello, John."

John is a big man, a bit overweight. He is about fifty-seven years old. He owns several stores, but he can always be found here, standing behind the counter with a cigar in the corner of his mouth. "I got a core cutter just the other day. It will drill holes in concrete floors up to twelve inches in diameter."

"Not today, John. I'm more interested in information." John sits down on the metal stool behind the counter and pushes his reading glasses up on his forehead. Tilting his head to the right with brows furrowed, John is intrigued.

"Like what?"

"Did you have anyone come in with a small case containing about forty pairs of good quality earrings?" John connects his inquiry to a recent one made by the police.

"Are these the same ones the cops are looking for?"

"Yes, those are the ones I'm asking about." Alexander notices John is distracted by Leslie's presence, and he's watching her.

"She's okay, John. She's with me."

John's attention returns to Alexander, and he speaks in a low tone, "Alexander you're putting me in an awkward position. I don't normally give out that kind of information. I respect the client-pawnbroker confidentiality and all that."

Alexander needs anything John can offer. "It's really important,

John; otherwise, I wouldn't ask."

John can tell Alexander is distressed, and he really likes this kid and his family. He also knows Alexander can be trusted. He pushes his glasses back down onto his nose. "Alexander, I don't know anything about them, but let me make a few calls. I'll reach out to your cell phone."

"Thank you, John, I appreciate that."

Alexander strolls over to where Leslie stands totally captivated by the store's contents. "See anything you like?"

"I like quite a few things, Alexander. There are items I can use at the studio. I'd like to come back at some point in time, but right now, I need to get back to my car so I can get home. I'm exhausted."

Leslie rides back quietly as Alexander heads to the studio. She feels content about the events of the day. It was a good diversion for her. Tomorrow she is determined to purchase an alarm system with video cameras and set up an installation date.

Alexander is feeling more confident that Leslie will not walk away from her business following their conversation inside John's pawnshop. He looks at her from the corner of his eye. "So Leslie, what is your plan?"

"Well, my first plan of action tonight is to get home and have a nice long bath followed by going to bed early. My more long range plan is to keep the design studio open. We worked too damn hard to let it go."

"I was hoping you would say that." Alexander's cell phone rings. "Hello? Okay, I won't say anything; you have my word, and I'm good for it." With that said, Alexander disconnects the call.

Leslie asks, "John?"

"Yes, one of the other pawnshops had the earrings from Allison's Jewelry Store brought in. It seems a man named Skunk brought them in."

Leslie is speechless. She has an eerie, anxious feeling. She needs to get home.

They pull into the parking lot of the Burlington Design Studio, and Leslie is wired to jump out. "Hey, what's the hurry?"

"I've had a long day today, Alexander, as I'm sure you have too. I guess I'm just overtired. I'll see you tomorrow." She kisses Alexander on the cheek and heads for her car.

Alexander isn't sure what is really on Leslie's mind, but he feels there is more to it than what she shared. "I'll probably come by early tomorrow if that's okay with you. I have a light schedule," he calls after her. Leslie smiles and waves. "That will be great."

3

6

Leslie is awake most of the night despite how tired she feels, and unfortunately, the hot bath did not help. She can't turn off her mind as she keeps putting pieces together, trying to make sense without much success. The night closes in, enveloping her, feeding on her insecurities. It is a restless night, one that she is happy to see end. Leslie needs to get to the studio. Her goal is purchasing a security system and setting up an install date.

Upon her arrival, Alexander is already there, standing outside the studio and smiling at her. "Good morning, Red."

"Good morning, Al. I'm so glad you're here. I have a few things to share with you that I should have told you about last night." Alexander is intrigued and, for the first time, feels he can exhale.

"I thought something was bothering you. I left here last night with an uneasy feeling." Leslie leads Alexander into her office, greeting Kathleen on the way, glancing into the kitchen to make sure the coffee is brewing. They take seats across from each other in the office.

Keeping her voice just quiet enough to ensure privacy, Leslie looks at Alexander. "The man that John said pawned the earrings, Skunk. I know him, or more accurately, I know of him." She has Alexander's full attention.

"How?"

"The other day when I went to Saint Gerard's to see Father Figuora, that man, Skunk, was on the street corner washing car windows for money."

"He got you, didn't he?"

"Yes, as a matter of fact, he did and it cost me five dollars, but that's not what's important. Father Figuora knows him and uses him to do odd jobs from time to time." Alexander closes his eyes and slowly shakes his head from side to side.

"Okay…but that doesn't mean anything sinister is going on." Leslie is impatient.

"Alexander, there is something there. I can feel it. I knew it when I gave Skunk the five dollars and he said thank you, sweetie."

"And?"

"Wait…wait, when I was in Father Figuora's office, he called me sweetie too. I can count on one hand the number of times a stranger called me that, and it's never happened from a priest. They just wouldn't do that." Alexander isn't completely sold on her suspicions, but he has to admit several coincidences bother him.

"I'm going to agree that maybe there is something there. I'm thinking it's looking like he is the person who robbed the jewelry store." Leslie sits forward,

"There is something else. What two things did Amy love above everything else?"

"Electronics and her Green Bay Packers."

"That's right! When we started this business, we purchased the best cell phone service we could afford with smart phones, but Amy still purchased her own smart phone with the NFL logo on it with the Green Bay Packers." Alexander nods.

"You're right, Red, but where are you going with this? That phone could very well be in her apartment."

"It's nowhere to be found. We found her work phone, but the Green Bay smart phone was always on her. I'm thinking, if Skunk has this phone, it would be the link from him to what happened at the studio that night."

Lost in their own thoughts, Alexander shares with excitement. "Tonight, you and I will stake out that intersection where you saw Skunk to see what he's up to. Maybe we'll even get lucky and spot him with Amy's phone. Have you told anyone else about this?"

"No, not yet, I just put those pieces together."

Alexander stands up to come around the desk where Leslie is sitting. "Let's hold off on telling anyone until we see what else we can find out. I'm going to go get some things done, but I'll be back to get you at 7:00 p.m."

Alexander hugs Leslie, and in an instant, he is gone. Leslie forces herself to stop thinking about their plans for this evening. She has to if she intends on getting any work done. She gets up, gets coffee, and starts her day by calling the security company.

Unfortunately the day drags for both of them. Normally they would complain about not having enough hours in a day. Today there is enough time to accomplish everything. It is 6:55 p.m., and Leslie is out of the studio in a flash. She crosses the parking lot, jogging toward Alexander's truck.

"Okay. Al, what's our plan?"

"We're going to go down by Saint Gerard's and park where we can inconspicuously watch Skunk. Here, I brought you a coffee. It may be a long night."

Alexander finds a place to park on a side street east of the intersection where Leslie had first spotted Skunk. Not only is the intersection in their full view but so is Saint Gerard's Rectory. Off in the background, lights flicker off Lake Champlain. Leslie's eyes scan back and forth.

"I don't see him."

"Give him a chance, Red. Stakeouts can take time."

Even though this section of town is in disarray, showing the signs of neglect, it is a busy area with people entering and exiting the rectory with what looked like bags of food. An hour later, a white Tahoe parks by the rectory's side entrance, and three boys climb out carrying boxes.

"Those boys are on the Saint Gerard football team. I recognize them from home games. Their well-known players who are pretty good, and they're the same boys Mrs. O'Brien said come to see Father Figuora regularly."

Just then Skunk comes out of the rectory's side entrance, carrying an army duffle bag. He crosses the parking lot and heads south toward the towns business district. Leslie is anxious to hop out of the truck upon Alexander's command.

"Are we going to follow him?"

"No, not tonight. Let's get a better feel for what's going on by staying so we can see what happens."

Less than twenty minutes later, Skunk returns empty handed and once again disappears through the side entrance of the rectory. It is puzzling.

"What do you think that's all about, Al?"

"Hard to say."

Another thirty minutes later, the boys and Skunk leave the rectory, get into the Tahoe, and exit the parking lot, making a left, this time heading north.

"Are we going to follow them?"

"No, I think I'm going to take a closer look."

"Al, I don't know about that. What if something happens? I don't like that plan." Alexander turns to face Leslie.

"Leslie, I promise I'll be careful. Keep the doors locked and be my lookout. I will be back in about fifteen minutes. I promise I'll be careful."

With that said, he hands her the keys and makes sure the truck is locked. He slides toward the rear of his vehicle and he is up the street and around the corner in no time. Leslie is uncomfortable about their adventure now that she is all alone. Uncertain about exactly how much time passed, she feels queasy. What exactly is she supposed to do as Alexander's lookout?

"Okay, Alexander, it's time for you to show yourself," Leslie states out loud.

As if he heard her, Alexander comes into view on the far side of the rectory. Moving quickly, he hides in the shadows by the side entrance. A moment later, he steps into the dull light and pulls something from his pocket. A few movements, and he quickly disappears inside. "And he can pick locks too…you learn something new every day."

Forty minutes later, Leslie begins to think something must be wrong. She slips out of the truck, locks the doors, and following Alexander's example, uses the shadows provided by the buildings to move toward the intersection. She barely reaches the corner when the white Tahoe returns and parks in the rectory parking lot once again. She sees the boys walk into the rectory. Without taking her eyes off of them, she backs slowly into a small alley to hide in the dark shadows. Her mind is racing, trying to determine what to do. Perhaps the best plan is to visit Father Figuora again.

Just as she is about to move, an arm wraps around her waist with a hand, covering her mouth. In a soft voice Alexander whispers, "It's me, Red." Alexander pulls her close to him in the shadows. She is shaking. Her heartbeat resonating to him. He can smell her hair, as his enthusiasm begins to build, Leslie turns to whisper, "Get in front of me, you devil."

He moves in front of her and shrugs. "Just happy to see you, but right now, we need to get out of here, Red. Stay in the shadows, and let's work our way back to the truck."

They make their way back up the street. Once inside the truck Alexander backs around the corner, turns the headlights on, and heads in the direction of the studio.

"I've got it, Leslie."

"What? You found Amy's phone?"

"Yes! There is a small room with a bed, computer, papers, and buckets with squeegees. That must be where Skunk stays."

"Did you find anything else?"

"A weight room, a food pantry, and several locked rooms."

"Don't tell me you had trouble picking those locks!" Leslie says in exaggerated shock.

"I might have been able to get into those rooms, but I needed to get out. It's a good thing too because, a few more minutes, and I would have come face-to-face with the three football players."

"Did you notice Skunk did not return with them?"

"I think we should call Youngblood and get him up to speed."

"No, Upton."

"Why him, Leslie?"

"He keeps calling me, wanting to know what I know, and he keeps telling me he's in charge. Frankly, Alexander, he scares me."

"All right, why don't you call him but don't tell him about the phone or John the pawnbroker."

Driving back to the studio, they wonder exactly what they've gotten themselves into. Once there, Alexander sits in the wing chair while Leslie calls Upton. Alexander is drawn out of his thoughts when the volume of Leslie's voice increases, and he hears her say, "Listen, Upton I also have someone who saw Skunk enter our studio that day… no, he doesn't want to be known at this time. I think you need to talk with Skunk." Leslie quickly hangs up the phone exhaling deeply. Alexander can tell she is frustrated.

"Why did you tell Upton that someone saw Skunk enter the studio?"

"Oh, he kept talking over me and saying you have no proof. I thought I might be able to force his hand."

"Do you think it worked?"

Leslie shrugs, "I don't know, but it did cause him to hang up on me."

Alexander thinks for a moment announcing, "I've got a guy…"

"What kind of guy?"

"He's a good guy. I'll have him sit on stakeout. It will give us the needed distance from visibility, and we'll go about our business as usual. This way, to the outside eye, everything looks normal, especially to Upton who we don't need poking around."

"You're right, Al. I think it's a smart plan."

Alexander stretches. "On a completely different note, how about dinner tomorrow night?"

"Sure… okay. Why are you looking at me like that?"

"Dinner is at my parent's house. They are dying to meet you, and I know you will love them as much as I do." Leslie feels both excited and nervous about dinner at his parent's home.

In that instant, she is back in the studio with Amy replaying their conversation about him. "All right, Al. I'll come but I can't leave the studio until 7:00."

"Not a problem, sweetie," he said, and with that, Alexander is on his feet, heading toward the studio door. Leslie shoots him a glaring look, but it didn't faze him. He loves teasing her.

7

Alexander shows up early at the studio. He decides to sit in his truck and watch Leslie as she reworks the display window. Leslie knows he's there but refuses to acknowledge him; she is annoyed.

She finds herself talking out loud to no one in particular. "Doesn't he own a watch? Perhaps if I buy him one he'll figure out how to be on time. I bet I could get a good deal on one from his friend John. Maybe I'll just have to do that."

Once vented, she feels somewhat better. When she's satisfied with the new window layout, she looks at him and waves him into the studio. Alexander enters, and Leslie looks up into his face with her hands down at her sides, palms up, fingers spread. "I'm pretty sure I asked you not to get here until 7:00 p.m."

"I know. I just couldn't be without you any longer, Red; and once I got here early, I decided to sit in my truck and watch you work. In fact, I'll just sit here in this chair and observe." Alexander plops down into the large wingback chair with crossed legs.

"Oh no, you don't. You're going to help me because, if we get married, this studio will be part yours. So there's no time like the present to get involved."

Leslie can't believe she just blurted that out. Up until this moment, their conversations never crossed over into this topic, and although she liked him very much, to blurt out something like that is so unexpected. Alexander is at a loss for words. His mind is scrambling to come up with something to fill the momentary silence when Sergeant Youngblood walks through the studio door. "Hello you two, how are you?"

Alexander is grateful for the distraction and marvels at his ability to time things so well. "I saw you and the coroner down by Lake Champlain this morning, sergeant. What did you find? A floater?"

"As a matter of fact we did. A homeless guy that's been around town for some time now. We don't know too much about him. He goes by the nickname Skunk."

Leslie's is shocked to hear this. Her mouth drops open, and she feels like she's been punched in the stomach. All she can do is look back and forth from Alexander to Youngblood.

"What's going on you two?"

Alexander asks the question burning to be answered, "What else do you know about Skunk?"

"He's one of the homeless seen around town who spends a good portion of his time around Saint Gerard's parish."

Alexander presses on, "Did Upton talk to you about him?" Youngblood is beginning to feel annoyed at the direction this conversation is taking after his mention of Upton.

"No, can't say he has, but I strongly suggest the two of you better start talking."

Urgently, the following words flood out from Alexander, "We believe Skunk killed Amy."

Youngblood's eyebrows raise, and he looks at them from one face to the other, exhaling loudly.

In the moments that follow, Alexander and Leslie fill him in on everything that led them to this conclusion. Youngblood stands there, engrossed by what he's just learned without sharing his thoughts. Alexander needs to know what Youngblood is going to do with the information about the pawned jewelry. After all, they have an allegiance with John and don't want to cause him any undue trouble. "I gave John my word his information will remain confidential. You're not going after him are you, Youngblood?"

"No, Alexander. John has always been pretty straight with me, but more importantly, do you have Amy's cell phone?"

"Yes, I have it in my purse." With that announcement, Leslie turns sprinting to her office to retrieve Amy's cell phone. Youngblood asks Alexander if they looked at her cell phone for any recent calls or her text messages to which Alexander confirms they had not.

Leslie is disturbed by the fact that this is the first time Youngblood is hearing anything about Skunk, and she wants him to know they did not tell Upton about their retrieving Amy's cell phone.

"Sergeant, why do you think Upton neglected to share with you what we told him about Skunk?"

Youngblood didn't need to discredit his fellow officer although it took great willpower not to. "I don't know. Leslie, it appears there is more here than meets the eye. First off, as I seem to recall, there is no mention of Amy having a second cell phone."

"Yes, that's true, but I just remembered the other day; and there seemed to be some really strange things happening around Saint Gerard's. We didn't leave it out on purpose, but I must admit, we didn't share that information with Upton either. You now know everything we do."

Youngblood understood their decision although he did not acknowledge his feelings. "Saint Gerard's adds a confusing element to this case, and I'm unsure to what degree or even if it's involved at all. Many diverse people are ministered to by the parish, and it adds many layers. It makes it difficult to determine who's involved. It's quite a conundrum."

Leslie is about to hand Amy's cell phone to Youngblood when it begins to ring. "I don't recognize the number. Should I answer it?"

Youngblood shakes his head no. "Someone is most likely looking for this cell phone for some reason. I'm guessing they want to find out who has it."

Leslie holds the cell phone out to Youngblood. "Then you answer it."

"No, I don't want to tip our hand. Let me have it checked out. I have someone I trust who can do it, and since no one knows about this cell phone, let's keep it that way."

Alexander's bond with Youngblood instantly increases, and he cannot resist teasing him. "Sounds dishonest to me, Harold."

Youngblood grins at Alexander and Leslie. Deep down, he really enjoys these two kids. "No, not really. If I bring the cell phone out now, you two might be placed in danger, and let's not forget the little matter of breaking and entering, Alexander."

Leslie asks the question she's sure crossed everyone's mind, "Do you think it's possible that Upton is involved?" Youngblood is not going to address this question directly.

"When I know something, I'll tell you both, but more importantly, you kids need to do the same." Leslie and Alexander both agreed to his request.

Harold turns Amy's cell phone off and places it in his inside jacket pocket for safe keeping.

"What would you like us to do?"

"For now, try to stay away from Upton as best you can; and, Leslie, it might be best if you did not stay alone at your apartment."

Leslie's not ready to leave her apartment. She just wants some type of normalcy. She knows he's right, but nonetheless feels deflated again. "Upton keeps pressing me for information. He's constantly telling me he is the man in charge."

Youngblood is not surprised. He knows he'll have to say something to Upton to get him to turn down his irritating behavior a few notches. "I'll tell Upton your parents came to me personally asking me to watch over you. That should back him off a bit. He doesn't know how to deal with important people, so we'll use that to our advantage."

"What about me, sergeant?"

"I don't believe you're in any personal danger, Alexander. At least not at this moment, plus I don't think anyone would volunteer to mess with you. It also doesn't hurt that you live on the property with your parents, and from what I hear, your father keeps his place locked down like Fort Knox."

Alexander agrees. "My father still lives in the past, and his primary philosophy is that it is easier to deal with life from a position of strength."

"I can't argue with that. I believe we can end up in trouble to a certain degree, but you're right in thinking things don't add up down there at the rectory. Here's the deal, when I have something, I'll call you but both of you need to stay away from the rectory for now. While you're at it stay away from the Upton too. If you need me, call." That being said, Youngblood takes off.

Both Alexander and Leslie are quiet for a while until Alexander declares, "I'm going back to the rectory." Leslie is shocked to hear him say that.

"No, you can't go back there, Al. You heard what Youngblood just said."

"I just need five minutes. There are papers in Skunk's room that I need to look at. There's some sort of schedule with dates and times. Plus, there is a computer. Why would Skunk need a computer?"

"Okay, Al, but let me call Youngblood…"

"Never mind; forget about it. Everything will be gone by now. There's no point in going. I just wish I had looked at that stuff." Alexander glances at his watch. "Isn't it closing time?" Leslie knows what that means, dinner with his parents. She is nervous about meeting them but one thing is for sure, she will learn more about Alexander.

They close the studio and climb into Alexander's truck. Leslie enjoys looking out the window and watches the beautiful countryside go by. Alexander makes a quick left down a dirt road. Leslie looks around. "We're not going deer hunting to get dinner first are we?" Alexander smiles at her. The ride into their property is really beautiful. "My family owns about two hundred acres."

The dirt road has two embedded tire tracks while the center is covered with patches of grass. The late afternoon brings darkness to the woods, revealing little along either side of the dirt road. Up ahead of them a rock wall comes into view similar to those seen in a farmer's field only taller. Another turn and they drive through an opening. The dirt road disappears, and they're now driving on a concrete driveway that circles around an ornate water fountain leading to a beautiful house constructed of field stone.

Their two-story home gives off a castle effect with its parapets and two mini towers at each end of the structure. As Alexander stops his truck, the front door opens and out rush four German Shepherds, making it almost impossible for Al to climb out of his truck. "Okay, okay, down! I love you guys too."

Al's Mom isn't far behind them. "Hello, Leslie."

Alexander's mom is a beautiful woman with salt-and-pepper hair and blue, blue eyes. She smiles, wiping her hands in her apron as she approaches her side of the truck. She gives Leslie just enough time to exit Alexander's truck before she greets her with a huge bear hug.

"Mom please put her down."

Leslie couldn't help but laugh. "Hello, Mrs. Acof. It is nice to finally meet you."

Mrs. Acof releases Leslie. "Please, call me Olga." She guides Leslie toward the open front door. Alexander follows.

"Is Dad home?"

"Yes, he's upstairs getting ready for dinner."

Leslie's happy to be here and all her prior reservations melt away. Their home is beautifully crafted, and Leslie can see where Alexander got his skill from. It's very different from the one she grew up in, which is also beautiful but never gave off the lived-in comfort felt here.

"Olga, you have a beautiful home." As Leslie crosses the threshold, she is in awe of the enormity. The entry area is larger than her entire apartment with two staircases winding their way up to the second floor. Olga watches Leslie as she takes in their home and smiles. "Would you like to freshen up before dinner, dear?"

"No, I'm fine, thank you."

"Then why don't we go into the dining room. Dinner will be out shortly. I'm a little off on the timing, so we need about twenty more minutes."

Dinner goes extremely well. The food is delicious, and the night is filled with good conversation and laughter. Leslie thinks it comical that the Acofs are Russian, but their home is decorated with French provincial furniture and a few English pieces while dinner was corned beef and cabbage.

It got late quickly without them even realizing how much time has passed. The Acofs invite Leslie to stay for the night. Alexander loves his parents offer almost as much as he loves them. "Leslie, why worry about going home? The studio opens at 10:00 a.m., so we can swing by your apartment for a change of clothes, and I'll drop you off at work."

"You talked me into it. I'll stay. Mrs. Acof, your dinner was delicious. I just love your home. This wallpaper is not from around here, and I've never seen a more beautiful chandelier."

"Thank you, dear. I do love to decorate. I'm glad you enjoyed dinner. Alexander, why don't you show Leslie to the guestroom? I'll have breakfast ready in the morning. Good night, Leslie."

"Good night, Mr. and Mrs. Acof."

Alexander smiles at his parents, excusing himself he escorts Leslie out of the dining room and upstairs. He leads her to the door of the guestroom and pausing at the threshold pushes the door open for her. Leslie looks at Alexander and says playfully, "Don't be sneaking into my room tonight."

Alexander laughs. "Here, take Princess with you. I guarantee no one will enter your room."

Leslie looks down at his dog Princess who wags her tail in agreement. While she wouldn't mind Alexander sneaking in, she is conflicted, being raised to refrain from sex until marriage. It's one part of her Catholic roots that stuck with her although, in this day and age, it is hard to believe anyone still lived by it. Leslie finds pajamas and climbs into bed. She looks over at Princess using the command, "Princess, come."

The German Shepherd crosses the room and hops on the bed. "Down." Princess flops down next to Leslie, placing her head on her ankle, giving a heavy sigh, letting Leslie know she's content.

Leslie plumps her pillow, thinking how grateful she is to be without the need for pepper spray tonight.

Princess lifts her head and gives a throaty growl, staring at the door. Alexander's head pops in. "Just thought you'd like to know how no one can sneak up on you."

"Thanks, Al, for everything." Al steps back to close the door,

"Good night, Leslie. Good night, Princess." Princess's tail taps the bed as she wags it, and the door closes.

8

That same day, in another part of town.

TGIF Youngblood gratefully thinks and he exhales deeply.

Youngblood leans back in his desk chair in the crowded precinct bull pen. He looks over at Upton. He cannot shake the feeling Upton is hiding something, but first he needs to get his focus off Leslie and Alexander. The thought of Alexander brings a smile to Youngblood's face. He mumbles softly, "Now you'd make a good partner."

As he thinks about the best way to misdirect Upton, he's tapped on the shoulder. Turning in his chair, he sees Peggy, the top police computer tech assistant. "You need me, sergeant?"

"Yes." Youngblood opens the bag that holds the cell phone for her to look in. "I need you to pull whatever information you can off of this cell phone including any text messages."

"Do you want the phone dusted for prints?" Youngblood shrugs shaking his head no. "I believe the phone's compromised so I think dusting for prints is useless."

"Okay, rest assured I'll get whatever it has to offer from it. No problem." Peggy takes the bag from Youngblood, but before she leaves, he adds, "Here's the kicker. No one is to know about this, no one."

Peggy nods her head in agreement. "I can do that, sergeant. I may have to work after hours on it depending on who's around and what work we have." Youngblood understood.

"I'll owe you one, Peggy. Please keep the cell phone out of sight."

"No problem. You'll have it tomorrow."

Once Peggy leaves, Youngblood gets up and walks over to Upton. He is worried recent rumors about Upton may be true, increasing his dislike for the man. He isn't one to pass on rumors until they became fact, but it's getting more difficult to push the recent rumors from his mind.

"Charles?" Upton looks up in disgust, "Well, look who it is, Mr. Goody Two-shoes."

"Can I sit down?" Youngblood asks, ignoring his last comment.

"Look, it's not Sunday so spare me any sermon you may want to add on to the last one."

"No sermon, it's the Amy Peters case…"

"Look, it's mine."

Youngblood held his temper. "Yeah, I know that but I just got a call from Mr. and Mrs. Turner and they asked me to check on Leslie as a favor to them."

"I don't give a rat's ass what they want. Stay out of it, Youngblood, or shall we go talk to the captain?"

"You just don't get it, Upton. There's no need to talk with the captain, but if you want to, we can. The Turner's wanted to call the captain and request I check in on Leslie, but I talked them out of it by telling them it wouldn't be a problem, but if you think you know better, it's entirely up to you."

"Have I called you a pain in my ass today?" Upton spits out. Youngblood can tell he's really pissed but he looks him in the face and shrugs.

"Not yet, but the day is still young."

Shoving his desk drawer closed with a loud thump, Upton exhales loudly. "Must you be involved in everything around here because, I can assure you, I've been doing this job for a long time before you came along."

Youngblood moves forward to the edge of his chair and, in his most empathetic voice, says, "Look, Charles, it's still your case. I'm just giving you a heads-up. I didn't think you would care if I checked up on Leslie and Alexander from time to time. I don't see any reason to get the captain involved. Plus if we do, you never know what his reaction will be or what will happen."

Charles sits there without saying a word. Youngblood figures he's listening to that little bird in his head sing. Upton exhales for the second time, making him think he should be checked for an air leak. "That better be it."

"Look, Charles, I may be able to help with babysitting the kids, that's all. It seems they trust me, maybe even extract some information out of them for you. At least that's what I'm thinking."

Youngblood can almost hear the gears grinding in Charles's head. He hopes he successfully sold this idea well enough for Charles to go for it. "Youngblood, you're still a big pain in my ass."

Youngblood takes this as an affirmative and stands up to leave. "Good, Charles, you back off of the kids; and if I get anything, you will be the first to know."

"Yea yea. Don't fuck with me on this, Youngblood. You can play with the kids but that's it. Understand?" Youngblood is somewhat shocked and relieved Upton buys his involvement. The fact that he gets a concession out of him makes him think he should give him something in return.

"The other reason I came over here is to ask you something." Youngblood has his full attention. "Did you know Amy Peters had a separate cell phone in addition to her work cell phone?" Upton eyes Youngblood, sizing him up. Keeping his body language relaxed, he can tell Upton is curious about how much he actually knows by the same token he's worried this much thinking on Upton's part could actually hurt the poor guy.

"Yea, they told me about her cell phone, but I didn't say anything because I figured the murderer probably has it. I'm setting a trap for him. That's why I didn't say anything. Is there anything else they know?"

"That's it. They're both still in shock, so for now that's all I've got. I just want to make sure you know."

Upton stares up at him, standing next to his desk. "Again, Youngblood, don't cross me on this."

Youngblood looks over the face of this Neanderthal who somehow retains his position of power on the force. He accomplished what he wanted to do and led him exactly where he wants him. "Charles, I'm not looking to cross you on this. But tell me how do you set a trap for the murderer when you don't have her cell phone?"

Upton's anger and his closed body language are telling him to walk away. "That cell phone is going to show up sooner or later, and whoever has it will be our man. Now, go to work and find it. I want that cell phone."

"When I come across it, it's yours." Youngblood slowly moves away from his desk. "That's right, Youngblood. You get to work and bring it to me. Right to me."

"I will, and if anything comes up pertaining to the kids, let me know."

Upton stands. "I've got it all under control. Now hit the bricks and get out of my sight."

Youngblood is through his office door in a flash, his mind sifting through what just took place when his desk telephone begins to ring.

He grabs the phone receiver. "Sergeant Youngblood." It's Alexander. "I'm putting you on hold, and I'll be right back." He moves into an empty office and pushes the office door closed for more privacy. "Hello, Alexander, what's up? Is there anything wrong?"

"Not exactly, sergeant, but early this morning, someone was on our property and tried to get into the house." Alexander had his full attention, pushing his conversation with Upton from the forefront of his mind.

"Did they get in?"

"No, my dad has a very good security system and our dogs scared them off."

Youngblood stands, his mind racing. "Do you need me to come up there?"

"No, thank you. Our carriage house is inhabited by two friends of my father; they're brothers. They live there as groundskeepers, but I believe they do more than that. I know I wouldn't want to run into them in the dark."

Youngblood nods his head remembering the two men. "I know the boys; your father has his own muscle, and that's okay. Old habits are hard to break."

"I'm not even sure they speak much English. My dad knows them from Russia."

"Rest assured, Alexander, I would never just drop in on your family without an invite. I know your property is like Fort Knox."

Alexander readies to terminate the call as he accomplished what he promised, keep Youngblood in the loop.

"Thanks for the information, Alexander. Have you heard from Leslie?"

"As a matter of fact, she stayed here last night. She's fine."

"Good. Keep an eye on her."

Alexander hangs up the telephone as Leslie walks into the kitchen with her new friend Princess walking right alongside her.

Alexander smiles and perks right up. "Can I offer you some eggs and bacon?"

"Nothing for me thanks. I had a wonderful sleep. Being here makes me feel so safe, and Princess sure is one wonderful dog."

In that moment, Alexander decides not to tell her what went on last night. He didn't want her to worry. "Well, in that case, let's get over to your apartment."

Leslie shakes her head no. Last night's sleep lasted longer than she planned. "Just drop me off at the studio. I'm showered, and your mom gave me clothes to wear. Plus it's late, and Kathleen will be waiting for me."

Alexander and Leslie say their good-byes, mentioning they'll be back tonight. Leslie is taken by surprise at this but does not let on. She plans on asking Alexander about tonight once they're alone. Alexander's parents walk with them out the front door and stand on the top step as they leave.

Alexander, Leslie, and Princess continue toward his truck. Once they are out of earshot, Leslie asks Alexander, "Why did you say we'd come back tonight, and why is Princess coming with us, Al?"

Al admires Leslie. She could have asked both questions earlier but she didn't, and she is intuitive enough to realize something is up. He's unsure how much information he's willing to share, but he begins with the most obvious, Princess. "First off, Leslie, my parents like you, and Princess is good to have around. I've got several things to accomplish today, so I'll be in and out of the studio. Princess is good company. Plus the added benefit is, in the event someone comes in that you're uncomfortable with, all you need to say to her, is the command watch."

Leslie had to admit she loves having her around. "She won't attack with that command will she?"

"No, with that command, she'll just watch; but if someone comes at you, just tell her to attack. Princess will not attack anyone unless you say the command watch first."

"Al, do you think this is really necessary?"

"I do, plus I want to respect my parents' wishes. Besides, Princess is my dog, and my mom is making one of her special dishes tonight, stuffed cabbage. She wants you to come back. Maybe it's all these years surrounded by men only, I don't know but she loves having you there." With that said, the three of them climb into the cab of his pickup, wave goodbye to his parents, and head out to the studio.

Kathleen is waiting. Alexander joins them in the studio for a quick cup of coffee as his pretext while his real mission is to look around. It's obvious to Leslie what he's doing, but she doesn't think Kathleen picks up on it. Alexander walks into Leslie's office. "Okay, why all the cloak and dagger, Al?"

Alexander plays dumb. "What. I just wanted to have a cup of coffee with you before we both begin our day."

Kathleen breaks in telling them the coffee is just about ready and to come and get it. With coffee in hand, they each sit down for some small talk before their days begin. Alexander finishes his cup and pushes his chair back from the table, "Well, I've got to go, but I'll be back." He grabs Leslie by her waist as Princess watches, kisses her, and heads for the door.

As the door closes, Leslie watches the stained glass create an array of colors and shapes on the studio floor.

9

Alexander is preoccupied with the recent events and his dislike for where things seem to be headed. As he passes the turn for work, his truck takes him in the direction of Saint Gerard's. He pulls up behind an unremarkable, nondescript pickup truck. He parks. Assessing the amount of foot and vehicle traffic, he waits a few moments until he's sure he can exit without a ripple. He hugs the passenger side of his vehicle and approaches the truck in front of him, hopping in.

Keeping his eyes forward, Alexander speaks to its occupant, "Hello Bert. I brought you some coffee and donuts." Bert is short for Bertoli. He is a longtime friend of the Acof family, and someone who's always there to help out anyway he can. Alexander did not know all the details of how his allegiance was formed with his father, but he knows he is someone they can trust. "Anything going on, Bert?"

Bertoli is digging into the donuts and sipping his coffee. "Thanks for the chow, Al. I was getting hungry. People go in and out all day long. That activity goes on every day with all the regular players except that big boy they call Rock."

"That's interesting. Rock's the center on the football team."

"Rock left the rectory first thing this morning, carrying the army duffle bag. I'm guessing it's like the one you saw Skunk with the other night. The only difference is I followed him."

Alexander's head shoots to the left. "I told you to stay put. We don't know what's going on, but if they see you or this truck, it could become a problem."

"Easy, Al. I followed him on foot by paralleling him using the next street up as my route. He walked downtown, made a left, and ended up coming right at me. As a matter of fact, he crossed the street within three feet of me."

"Did he look at you?" Alexander did not hide his intrigue.

"Nope. He never saw me. Rock was too concerned about what might be behind him. He went down another block and entered the Greyhound bus terminal."

"Were you able to see what he did once inside or who he met?"

Bertoli shook his head. "He met no one. He put the duffle bag into one of the bus terminal lockers. He stayed only a few minutes, just enough to do the deed, check his back, and he left. He worked his way back to the rectory, taking the long way."

"What was the locker number?"

"Eleven."

"And you're sure he never saw you?"

"I'm sure. He worked his way back using the next street over, and I hightailed it back to my truck. I sat here watching him come out of State Street then I saw him approach the intersection."

Alexander is grateful for the work Bert has accomplished. He decides it's time to give him a break to change his clothes and get a proper meal. "Why don't you take off for a while?"

Alexander hands him his keys. "Take my truck and be back by six."

"Al, is your old man going to be good with what I'm doing? Does he know?"

Alexander smiles at him. He knows Bertoli won't do anything to jeopardize his relationship with his family. He realizes he's put him in a tough spot.

"I'm sure he'll be fine with it. My plan is to explain what we're doing tonight at dinner. I promise I'll take care of it. Now take off, Bert, and thanks."

Bertoli uses his best Arnold voice, "I'll be back." He chuckles. "I always wanted to say that." He exits his vehicle noiselessly and disappears.

Alexander hears the whine of his reverse gear as Bert backs up around the corner followed by the sound of that big block fade off into the distance. Alexander appreciates the quiet. His eyes scan the intersection and the rectory parking lot. He watches as the boys come and go, bringing boxes and bags, occasionally returning with a stranger only to leave with that stranger on their next trip.

The activities feed Alexander's desire to get inside the rectory, but the risk of being seen is too great at this time of day or, could be much worse, getting caught. He needs a lookout. He knows Leslie is right. There is definitely more going on here, but the question is, how much more?

His legs begin to cramp. He needs to stretch them soon. Six o'clock rolls around. Alexander can hear his truck off in the distance growing louder as it gets closer. It brings a smile to his face. He thinks about how his dogs always know when he gets home. He decides he should get a new truck just to screw them up.

Bert parks Alexander's truck behind him. He waits until the traffic dies down before he climbs out to join Alexander. Bert slides in from the passenger side, and he looks over at Alexander. "Well?"

"You were right, Bert. People in and out the whole time you were gone. Some faces I had never seen before. I don't know what to make of it." Bert nods his head in agreement.

"How late tonight?" he asks.

"Why not break off about midnight? I don't think we need anymore. I'll call you tomorrow. Good with you, Bert?"

"Sounds good to me."

Alexander disappears into his truck and takes the same exit route used earlier by Bert and heads for the studio. He is determined to have Leslie stay at his parents' home. There is plenty of room and his parents really like her, but most of all, he knows she will be safe there. Alexander pulls up and parks, watching as the two girls go back and forth, focusing on something. He can tell they will most likely be busy for a while working.

It isn't too much past seven when Kathleen walks out the front door. She waves hello to Al, and he hears her tell Leslie he's out front. He watches her get in her car and pull away from the studio.

Alexander enters the studio and sits in his favorite wing chair. He likes this chair because it is man size. Leslie joins him, sitting in a smaller version of his chair. Alexander looks her over.

"You look tired, honey."

Leslie shrugs. "I'm not really tired, Al. I just can't get Amy out of my mind today."

"I know. You miss your partner."

Leslie makes a sweeping motion with her arms, taking in the vastness of their studio. She exhales a deep sigh.

"This was her baby, Al. I mean, I wanted this too but she fought for it. She never took no for an answer, and she always spoke confidently about what we needed to do. I always felt like it was a sure thing. Amy was the business savvy part of this operation."

Alexander kept quiet. He's glad she's finally talking about Amy. "When we were looking for a location, she said we needed one that benefitted from both foot and vehicle traffic. She was determined to find a location with a large display window we could fill with our interior concepts as if on stage to attract high end customers. There are a lot of career people in this area. When this location opened up it was perfect. We're close to Church Street, which attracts lots of people, and Main Street is the primary road used in this area by many people."

Alexander nods agreement. "You're right. The traffic in this area sure does slow me down." Leslie smiles at him for lightening up the moment.

"Amy wanted a location not far from the many beautifully manicured Victorian homes." Leslie's eyes fill with tears, and Alexander holds her hand.

"Red, are you sure you need to do this to yourself?"

"I miss Amy. I was so lucky to have her as my best friend, and I miss her so much. It really bothers me that we don't know what happened and why." Alexander stood.

"Let's call it a day. Come home with me tonight."

"No, not tonight but thank you for everything. I need to be home in my apartment tonight."

He understood plus he didn't want to be the source of added pressure. They lock up the studio, set the newly installed alarm, and climb into his truck. On the drive over to her apartment, Alexander stops at one of their favorite burger places. During dinner, he attempts to gently dissuade her from staying alone tonight but drops it quickly. He will have Princess stay tonight.

The one thing neither of them enjoyed is finding a place to park at her apartment. There are never enough parking spaces for the residents. Alexander stops in front of her building, looking for a spot. "I'll just get out here, Al."

"No, I'll feel better seeing you into your apartment, and I'm leaving Princess with you tonight." With that said, Al double-parks his truck. Locking the doors, he grabs Princess's leash.

Leslie opens her apartment door, smiling at Al. She is grateful he's so protective. She loves the thought of Princess staying with her. It makes her feel secure. One glance inside and Alexander grabs Leslie's arm pushing her out of the way. The apartment has been ransacked.

Alexander takes Princess off her leash and commands her to scout the apartment. She takes to the task at hand only to return, giving them the signal the apartment is clear. Leslie and Alexander step into the apartment, taking in all the chaos. Leslie looks up into Alexander's face, revealing her concern and confusion. "Why would anyone do this, and what can they possibly be looking for?"

Alexander shakes his head. "I don't know the answers, but we need to call Youngblood."

It didn't take long for Youngblood, who wasn't far from their location, to arrive in mere minutes. He works his way through the apartment and, when finished, turns to the kids asking, "Can you tell if anything is missing?" Leslie cannot.

Alexander is angry and thinks he might know the reason behind this destruction. "It's that dam cell phone, isn't it, sergeant?" Leslie loses her last shred of secure feelings. She is very aware that the chill has returned. Youngblood thinks the cell phone angle is a real possibility. "I think you may be on to something, Alexander. Someone is doing their best to retrieve it."

Leslie did not put up a fight when Alexander tells her she is not spending the night in her apartment. She quickly grabs her weekender bag to fill it. Alexander suggests she take enough clothes to last her a week. She grabs Princess as she heads for the bedroom.

Youngblood agrees that this is a good idea. Driving to his parents' home Leslie is silent. She experiences those old feelings she felt when her parents ran her life. It is hard to accept the thought that her life is no longer her own yet again. Alexander turns on a dirt road. Leslie can't see anything from the side windows of the truck due to darkness. The only thing visible is through the front windshield because of the headlights. It's like she's in a black-and-white movie. Alexander drives through the opening in the rock wall where there stands a mountain of a man.

"Who is that?"

"That's Karl, our grounds keeper." Karl looks down at them as they pass through the gate, showing no emotion, just a cold stare.

Alexander's truck hits cement pavement and the ride becomes smooth and quiet. The only sound small pebbles becoming free from the tire treads hitting the inside wheel well.

Alexander stops the truck, and Leslie sees his mom standing there as she had the night before with a big grin on her face. The front doors wide open, spilling the inside light out on the steps. Sitting next to her is a big German Shepherd.

10

Leslie awakens to Princess's throaty growl followed by a knock on the guest bedroom door. It's not very loud, just loud enough to be heard. "Can I come in?" It's Alexander.

"Yes, please enter." Leslie is a queen sleeping in this enormous room complete with a fireplace, a canopied bed, a beautiful sitting area with two wing chairs separated by a table, leading to french doors and a balcony.

Alexander comes in closing the door quietly behind him. As he approaches, Princess's tail beats against the bed. He grabs her muzzle and scratches the top of her head then walks over to one of the wing chairs and sits down. "Did you sleep well?"

"Like a baby. Thanks for asking. It's been so long since I slept this well."

"We're about to have breakfast, and I'm thinking we should walk to the lake since it's a beautiful day outside. What do you think?"

Leslie loved the idea. "Do I have time for a shower?"

"Yes, you sure do. I'll meet you downstairs." Princess never moves even as Leslie gets out of bed. Leslie stretches and looks around, saying to her, "This is some house you live in."

A short while later, Leslie and Princess join everyone in the dining room. There is a boisterous conversation going on, and everyone turns to greet Leslie as she enters the room simultaneously, saying good morning. Urie, Alexander's father, rises as she enters the room to guide her to a chair. "I hope you like waffles. We have the best Vermont maple syrup, and you have the benefit of selecting from four different flavors. My wife and I like the fancy grade A, and Alexander prefers grade B. To him it's thicker and more flavorful, but the trick here is to test them all to determine which one is for you."

It's as if the cook is waiting for this queue, and he rolls in the cart with plates of waffles for everyone. Leslie is impressed. Even the dishes are heated. There is whipped cream, powdered sugar, and strawberries. Leslie is in the process of sampling her first syrup selection when Karl, the man she saw last night, walks into the dining room. He asks them to excuse the interruption and moves over to where Urie is sitting, handing him a piece of paper.

Leslie looks from Karl to the image of a man outside the dining room's french doors and back to Alexander. He understands her confusion. "This is Karl who we saw last night, and that man outside the house is also Carl with a C. They are twins. Both take care of the grounds along with other miscellaneous jobs." Leslie smiles and leans in close to Alexander saying, "I guess that's better than being named Darrell and Darrell." Alexander grins.

Olga, Alexander's mom, asks them, "What are you kids up to today?"

"We think we'll take a hike up to the lake since it's so beautiful out."

Olga grins. "That's a great idea, plus the dogs can use the exercise."

Urie turns to Leslie and asks her the question he hopes will elicit a positive response. "Leslie, Alexander tells me you'll be staying with us for a while." Leslie blushes. She is so grateful to them for opening up their home to her but is embarrassed to bring her troubles into their lives. "I would love to if that's no bother to you."

Urie smiles at her. He is glad she is staying. "Not at all, dear. We love having you here, and we hoped you would stay."

Urie looks at the paper Karl gave him and announces, "I need to take care of something. Please excuse me everyone. I'll be back shortly."

Breakfast is finished, and Olga suggests they leave for their hike. She knows Urie will be tied up for a while, and she doesn't think they should wait for his return. Alexander grabs Leslie's hand and they leave with the dogs in tow.

The morning air is crisp and feels good. The sun casts shadows around the trees, but the early morning color is lost. The trail gradually inclines. It's made up of ATV tread marks and horse hoof prints. Leslie loves being out here and enjoys the quiet. She watches the four dogs run up in front of them, turn back, making sure they're coming, and run off again.

"I feel honored having these four dogs looking out for us. I feel like royalty."

"You don't know how right you are. You know Princess and the big male is King, next to him is Queen, and the one leading us and running wild is Duke." Leslie laughs out loud. "See, I knew I was right. Royalty."

The smells, sights, and freedom of being outside in nature are so beautiful. Leslie and Alexander enjoy their decision to hike, each of them lost in their own thoughts. They are in synch. Alexander shares, "This is where I come to think."

"It's so beautiful, Alexander. The only sound is the occasional bird, and Duke running around out there."

"Duke is the one who gets into everything." As the trail crests, it reveals the twenty-acre lake. Alexander points to a small cabin he built to their left. "That's the cabin I built. It's little but the porch is perfect, and it faces the lake. There's no electricity, but the chairs are comfortable, and it's a great place to sit and think."

Leslie loved it. "Thank you, Alexander, for sharing your special spot with me."

"I keep the cabin stocked with bottled water, canned goods, and dog food so I can stay all day or even overnight." Leslie liked the look of the cabin. It was only 16 by 16 feet, but the surroundings made her think of Switzerland. Alexander retrieved the chair cushions from the cabin, and they both settled in to soak up Mother Nature.

"Al?"

"Yes."

"Why did your parents come to the US?"

"My father's been in construction his whole life even in Russia. He had a good-size construction firm that did very well. Life was good according to him until certain families and the government began to try to extract money from him."

"Was life there that corrupted?"

"Yes, unfortunately it was. To survive, my dad had to align himself with one of the controlling families. As time went on, my dad actually became good friends with them. Eventually, my father took the family into his business as a partner then ended up selling the business to them."

"Is that why you left, Al?"

"No, I had an older brother named Dimitri. He worked for my dad too. One day, Dimitri was taking a payoff to a local union. He had to grease wheels to get a job up and running. It was a huge project, the size of the mall in Minnesota."

"Mall of America?"

"Yes, pretty much, but maybe a little less grand. Anyway, these two employees belonging to another family got wind of this, and they robbed Dimitri and took his life."

Leslie's eyes fill with tears. Alexander, like her, understood the loss of a loved one before their time. "I'm so sorry, Alexander."

"I was only eleven at the time."

"What happened to them? Were the police able to get them?"

"The police couldn't. They were protected so my father took care of it." Leslie covers her mouth with her hand, "Oh my god."

"I'm not supposed to know but he had to get out of the country. There is a price on his head. That's why he sold his business to his partner. They're still in touch and Dad uses him from time to time. Not only is this guy a mob boss, but he's got connections with the KGB."

"Is that where the 'bookends' come in?"

Alexander laughs. "You mean Carl and Karl? Yes, they were only twenty-one-years-old at the time. They had no family. My dad's partner insisted dad take them with him."

"Oh my, Al! Did anyone try to get to your father or try to stop your family from leaving?"

"In the beginning, but the bookends squelched it, and my dad's partner made that family pay dearly for the attempt."

Their conversation stalls. The day drifts on leisurely while they talk about everything as the sun touches the horizon. Alexander stands and begins to gather everything up. "We need to get back." Leslie is concerned about walking down the trail in the dark forest cover. Alexander can tell Leslie is not looking forward to the walk back to the house.

"Don't worry, we're fine. We have the dogs and one of the Karl's is always near."

Leslie is taken aback. "Is Karl here now?"

"I don't think so, but I'm sure he was here. I know it sounds strange and honestly it takes a little getting used to especially when you're somewhere and you think you're alone and the next thing you know Karl is next to you."

"Which Karl?"

"It's hard to tell even after all these years. When we say Karl it covers both of them."

They made good time going off the mountain. As they approach the house, all four dogs leave them behind, rushing forward and positioning themselves for entering the kitchen door. It is clear they know it's dinner time.

As they enter the kitchen, Alexander asks his mom, "What's for dinner?"

She is dressed in her familiar way, in a dress with an apron, which Leslie is getting used to. She is bustling around the kitchen, chopping things and stirring pots filled with delicious smelling ingredients.

"Spaghetti and meatballs; your father's favorite."

"Figures."

11

The following morning, Alexander and Leslie get up early to head into the studio. Leslie did a lot of thinking before she fell asleep the night before. This is the best time to share her concerns with Alexander, now that they are alone.

"You know, Al, I think we've gotten ourselves caught up in something. I just don't understand what it is."

"I think we might be about to find out what. There's Youngblood parked in front of the studio."

Alexander parks in the lot, and they walk toward the front door of the studio. Leslie opens the door, deactivates the alarm as Youngblood follows them in. Leslie speaks first to Youngblood.

"Good morning, sergeant. How about some coffee?"

"That sounds good. Then we need to talk."

Kathleen comes in behind Youngblood and, overhearing Leslie, offers to make the coffee. They move up front behind the display window, which is now like their little office. The two wing chairs have the addition of a coffee table placed between them. Alexander pulls over a third chair from the display window, which Youngblood takes from him to sit on. Alexander looks at Youngblood. "What's up, sergeant?"

"I did a check on Skunk, and I was able to get prints off his body. It seems Skunk's real name is Joseph Candelara. He is out of California in the Los Angeles area. The police have been looking for him. He was a big drug coordinator out there. I say coordinator because he acted as the man who got the drugs to different distributors. He dealt directly with the drug lords, which they suspect are located in Mexico. Sonora, Mexico, to be exact."

"So are you saying the drugs are now coming through Burlington?"

"Yes, it appears so."

Youngblood looks for their reaction, but nothing comes from either of them. All three get lost in their own private thoughts, trying to make some sense out of what is behind the killing of Amy and how drugs could possibly tie in.

"You know, sergeant, that night when I was in the rectory, there were all types of bus schedules. I also remember seeing a board hanging on the wall filled with numbers from one to twenty and boxes to the right of the numbers. In the boxes were time schedules and other numbers or letters that made no sense to me. What do you think? Could that be some type of delivery schedule?"

"I'm not sure, Alexander, but things are slowly falling into place. I'm not done with Joseph Candelara yet. You know how someone is always trying to cut in to someone else's turf? Well, this Mexican gang tried it, and Joseph was fingered as the one who took out some of his rivals. It's not real clear yet how he escaped prosecution, but somehow, he ended up here."

"So he must have had strong ties to someone."

"I think so. He's definitely not on his own. He's a soldier not a general, and his drug habit was fueled by his leaders to keep him in line like a puppet."

Leslie thought about what Youngblood shared. It is frightening. "So Skunk came here to continue whatever work they had planned for him, and he was able to be very low key. I mean, what is more invisible than a homeless person?"

Youngblood agreed. "He was most likely brought here for his talents."

Leslie thought back to her last visit with Father Figuora. That is the same day she met Skunk. She still felt uncomfortable. "Is it possible that Father Figuora is more involved than just helping out the homeless? Is it possible he was Skunk's boss?"

Youngblood shifts in his seat. He is surprised how smart both of these kids are, and Leslie's last comment confirms what he's been thinking. "That is a possibility. There are not enough known facts for me to stamp him a drug boss, and with his vocation, we have to tread carefully. I did go down to the morgue for a second time to look over Skunk's body. The one thing that stayed with me was his tattoos. One in particular is the one on his forearm. It's a cross with a serpent wrapped around it, and on the cross is the number eighty-two."

Alexander sits forward in his chair, barely able to keep back his excitement. "That numbering I told you about on the board in the rectory, it's possible it ties into the number on the tattoo? What if they are using numbers in place of a person's name?"

Kathleen brings them coffee and donuts. They exchange some pleasantries, and she leaves them to get to work. Once she's gone, Youngblood sets up some ground rules with urgency. He second guesses whether or not he has drawn them in too far by being too frank. "The bottom line is, I need more information, but first I want you kids to stay out of this. I need you to promise me that the rectory is off limits."

Leslie doesn't want to make this promise to him. She has too much invested in finding out who killed her best friend. "If Father Figuora is the drug boss then he can be the person responsible for Amy's death."

"Sergeant, we admit you've been very good to us, but I have to admit I have someone staking out the rectory. There are people constantly coming in and going out of there all day long. They carry boxes and army duffle bags, returning at times, empty handed or just empty. In fact, twice that we know of, the duffle bags were placed in lockers at the Greyhound bus terminal."

"Did you see who picked the contents up?"

"No. Our interest is what's going on inside the rectory. Leslie had a gut feeling right from the beginning bad things were going on in there."

Youngblood looks back and forth at the faces of both kids. "Before

I go, I need a promise that the rectory is off limits to you."

Leslie and Alexander answer in unison, "Okay, we promise."

Youngblood shares what he's learned about Father Figuora. "I also did a check on Father Figuora. He's been with the church since his altar boy days. His mother's in California near Santa Rosa. She's in a nursing home with advanced Alzheimer's disease. That's about all I have on his family so far."

Leslie is intrigued by his work and she has a new found fondness for Youngblood. "Sergeant, Father Figuora's been in our parish four or five years. Were you able to find out where he was before this?"

"Our Lady of the Sacred Heart in Sonora, Mexico, is what I've been told…"

Leslie's hand goes up to her mouth involuntarily. "Oh my god, Sonora, Mexico! That can't be a coincidence."

"If you think that's suspicious, I've got more. While dealing with the police down in Sonora, which is no easy undertaking, I learned many of them knew Father Figuora. His reputation is one of a well-respected man who did great things for the communities he served. The only mystery is the timing around his leaving although I'm not sure what happens behind the scenes when this type of instruction is given to a priest."

Leslie is listening to him, but it conflicts with what her intuition tells her. She shakes her head. "No…there's something about him that is just not right."

"You've got to listen to her, sergeant. When Leslie feels things, she is usually right on the money."

"I know how she feels. I also asked about anything else happening at the time Father Figuora was transferred up here. The one huge headline was the assassination of one of the biggest drug pins. It wouldn't have caught my eye as suspicious except for the fact that a large part of Father Figuora's focus was working against this man. His name was Tomas Garcia."

"Do you think there is a connection between Father Figuora and what seems to be going on up here?"

"It's possible; it's very possible. There are too many coincidences; it's Occam's razor. The way I heard it, Garcia's car was fire bombed, went off the road into a creek of about two to three feet of water. Everything burned except whatever was submerged. They said the body was burned up beyond recognition. So the coroner did nothing to confirm it was actually him. Another interesting piece of information is the fact that it was common knowledge he had tattoo's everywhere as well as all the men associated with him."

Leslie speaks in a quiet, trancelike tone, "Garcia is still alive."

Youngblood looks at her, sizing up her intuitive skills. "They believe so, but he's not down there living a happy life as far as they know, and they have no plans on trying to find him. Oh, and one last thing, Amy's cell phone, the only number that didn't belong to her was a number in Mexico. They're working on tracing who the number is connected with and giving me that information. Listen, kids, I'm not trying to scare you, but it's time to be smart. Leslie, I don't want you alone at your apartment. I need you to continue staying at the Acof's home. It's really the safest place in town right now. I'm also giving Amy's cell phone to Upton."

Leslie is breathing fast and shallow. "I don't like Upton, and he's been calling me every few days asking me about the craziest things. The cell phone is one of them. He will be glad you give it to him, but what are you going to tell him when he asks where you got it from?"

"I plan on making something up like I found it in one of the evidence bags hidden behind some of the other stuff. I'll think of something. If he's so anxious to get his hands on it, I'm confident he won't think twice about whatever I tell him. There's something manic about how bad he wants that cell phone."

Youngblood is ready to make tracks and he stands up. "No rectory, you gave me your word. If you guys go near the rectory, it can get you in trouble; and if anything comes back on me, I can lose my job."

Alexander stands to shake Youngblood's hand. "We won't go near the rectory, we promise."

12

Youngblood pulls up to the precinct, parks his car, and takes a minute to look around and appreciate the day. It's sunny out, and he sure would like to be anywhere else. He thinks about fishing. Then he sees Upton's cruiser. He needs to talk with him, but his distaste for Upton fills him with anger. Youngblood takes a deep breath of fresh air and exhales, completely emptying his lungs. He's resigned himself to getting this talk done. Pushing through the front door, he heads right for Upton's desk.

Upton's jacket is off and his white shirt shows sweat stains. Youngblood approaches him with Amy's cell phone inside a brown lunch bag. "I already had breakfast."

"It's the cell phone you've been looking for." Upton looks at Youngblood and opens the bag to look inside.

"Where, may I ask, did you get this? How did you get this and when?" Youngblood's face does not give away anything he does not want Upton to see.

He looks back at this man he can't stand and replies, deadpan, "I put the word out I was looking for the cell phone. This morning when

71

I got into my truck, it was on the front seat."

"Really… just like that and, bingo, it was on your front seat?" Upton is shaking his head in disbelief.

"You know what, Youngblood? You continue to be a royal pain in my ass."

Youngblood stares at him in disbelief, standing with his hands open and his shoulders high. "I know you want to find the cell phone, so I reach out to all my CIs. So here's the cell phone, and I'm a pain in your ass?"

"The fact that one of your CIs gives you the cell phone means they're involved. They know how hot this item is, and they can very easily be the murderer, but they just hand the cell phone over to you. Kind of convenient, if you ask me."

Youngblood is so frustrated he can spit. "No, Charles, a murderer wouldn't risk being seen dropping off the cell phone in a cops truck. They would dispose of it, drop it in Lake Champlain, or something like that. God, Charles, you are unbelievable." Youngblood turns to walk away. He needs some space.

"And you got it this morning, is that what you're selling?"

Youngblood looks at him. "Yes, Charles, that's what I'm selling."

Upton's anger is apparent, but Youngblood can't figure out exactly why. "Tell you what, Youngblood; I lost my fuckin' car keys the other day. How about putting that out there for me?"

Youngblood moves back in the direction of his desk again. "Can do, Charles, but I'm confident once they find out the keys belong to you, they will end up at the bottom of Lake Champlain."

Youngblood feels extreme satisfaction, and he smiles at Charles as he walks away backward. Charles looks away, pulling the cell phone from the bag.

"I guess you don't care about adding your prints to it, huh, Upton?"

"So you're telling me you didn't touch the phone?"

"That's what I'm telling you. You said you wanted it. As soon as I got my hands on it, and I brought it right to you."

"Then I'll take it from here. Now get lost."

"Sure thing, Charles. Remember keep me in mind if you need

help."

Youngblood didn't wait for an answer and is not surprised when one is not forthcoming. All he hears is a grunt. Youngblood had to admit he felt better than he did a few minutes earlier before their chat. He maneuvers over to his desk and sits down.

He thinks about how much he's confided in Leslie and Alexander. Some would see this as unprofessional, and he is torn about how to feel. He will work on not doing it again hopefully. He knows that if the captain gets wind of what he's shared with them, he will be in big trouble. He just likes those two. They're both hardworking and it's refreshing. Too often, he runs into kids who feel they're entitled to cars, money, and lots more from their parents. These two earn what they have, and if he is being honest with himself, this investigation would not have gained so much momentum if not for them.

A smile returns to his face. He likes having these kids close to him, and he needs them close because they need his protection even though he can't pinpoint exactly why yet.

Youngblood watches as Upton stands, puts on his jacket, and drops the cell phone in his jacket pocket. It's clear he's heading out, and he needs to know where. Youngblood pretends to be busy, engrossed in the paperwork on his desk; but once Charles leaves, he is going to follow him.

On the other end of town, Alexander is back on one of the side streets by the rectory. One thing is for sure, the food pantry and soup kitchen support a lot of foot traffic. Alexander fights the urge to reenter the rectory. It is overwhelming. If not for his promise to Sergeant Youngblood, he would be in there. As he sits there watching the activity, he spies Detective Upton pulling into the rectory's parking lot and entering the side entrance.

Alexander wonders why Upton is at the rectory. There must be a new development in the case that brought him here. Deep in thought, he is startled when his passenger door opens and Sergeant Youngblood slides in. "I thought we had an agreement."

"I'm not inside the rectory, so I'm thinking no harm, no foul."

"You have a point, but I thought it was understood you are to stay clear of this area?"

"Upton just went in there."

"I know. I followed him here. I gave him the cell phone this morning, and he made a beeline for the rectory. Pretty interesting, don't you think?"

"Do you think he bought your story about how you got the cell phone?"

"He's a complicated man. I'm unsure about whether or not he bought my story. But one thing I know for sure is you need to get out of here now."

"I've been careful. There's been another delivery to the bus terminal." Alexander knows Youngblood is angry with him, and he can't afford to lose his support. His heart tells him it is wrong to be there.

"Okay, sergeant, I'm leaving. No more side street parking either. I'll see you later."

They say their good-byes and both of them leave the area.

13

The kitchen is filled with the most delicious smells from Mrs. O'Brien's cooking. Father Figuora steps in for breakfast, and as he sits down to eat, his mind is focused on ten years earlier.

He is back in Sonora, Mexico. The Garcia brothers, Carlos and Tomas, were basking in the success of their lucrative drug trade that stems from Mexico into the Unites States. It isn't the biggest set up, but it keeps the Garcia's comfortable in a lifestyle they've grown to love.

Carlos is considered the brains of their operation. He has a knack for paying off the right people to look the other way. Plus the need for jobs in Mexico keeps the government out of their business even when they find proof to support taking action. The Garcias employ well over one hundred people in many towns and cities all over the country. Their mules move their product up into America using a tunnel they constructed over the years from Tecate, Mexico, to a small automotive garage outside Potrero, California.

Tecate, Mexico, is a perfect starting location filled with resort areas and tourist destinations. In general, the levels of drug-related violence and crime that are reported in the border region exclude this area from being considered a major trafficking route.

Potrero is Spanish for pasture land with Tecate, Mexico, being its closest neighbor. It has a land density of 3.1 square miles. The garage in Potrero is a small operation, keeping the farming and local vehicles in running condition. It houses a small fleet of vehicles for the drivers who take off from there, going in all directions. There are four major dispersion areas in the United States, and for the northeast, it is Albany, New York.

Part of their operating success is the use of a variety of inconspicuous routes. A driver can head up Route 15 to Route 70 where they have the opportunity to take various roads. The first stop is usually Denver where the mule is dropped off while another returns. The mule in Denver then finds his way to the bus terminal and heads east to Albany.

The Garcia's stay under the radar working, what the larger cartels consider a low-tech operation, which while true, runs smoothly. The Garcia's always work to keep the mules moving.

Life was beautiful for them until Father Frank Figuora transferred to Sonora in 2008. Father Frank worked his magic on the good people of Our Lady of the Sacred Heart. He made them see the evil of living a perverse lifestyle. He taught them to understand what is important and what's not. He had a way with people and their families, which influenced the downturn in drug use, causing some of the hardcore mules to turn to religion.

None of this sat well with the Garcias. Their well-established operation was falling apart, their product was not getting to where it had to go, and profits were down. They wanted and needed Father Figuora gone. The challenge became finding someone to make the good father disappear. It was nearly impossible. He was a saint in the area, and they had almost given up their quest until Carlos got wind that Figuora was being transferred to the United States. This was exactly what Carlos was looking for, and it could not have come at a better time.

The Sunday before he was scheduled to depart, the parishioners planned a party for the good father. It was on this very same day that Carlos instructed Tomas to enter the rectory to find out whatever information he could about his departure and destination. As it turned out, Father Figuora was being transferred to Burlington, Vermont, which was in close proximity to Albany, New York, where they had recently dispatched Skunk to find out why their profits in this area had fallen off so greatly.

Albany, New York, is their staging area for the drugs that come into the Northeast. Once there, the product is sent to Boston, New York City, Newark, and Philadelphia, just to name a few locations. The drugs come down to the major cities instead of up to them from Mexico, employing this unexpected route that the DEA has not yet discovered.

The night Tomas entered the rectory he learned lots of good information just as Carlos anticipated, like in less than one week, Father Figuora would be gone. Tomas remembers that night like it was yesterday. At first he had balked at Carlo's plan to cut his hair, add glasses, and practice a few mannerisms well known to Father Figuora. Initially, he just wanted to let the good father leave, but Carlos was adamant. He wanted him to pay for what he had done to their business over the last few years. Plus with Skunk in the area, it was a winning plan.

It was in that moment that he said good-bye to Tomas Garcia, and he and Carlos toasted the long life of Father Figuora. Carlos is his older brother. He learned to accept the fact that he was the enforcer and a great hit man. He had no guilt over doing dirty deeds.

Looking back, he realizes the plan's timing was genius since the police were closing in on him after all these years. Even if proof was hard for them to come by, it became progressively harder for witnesses to keep quiet. Thanks to Father Figuora. Once they killed off Tomas, the Mexican authorities would focus on other things.

The other portion of this plan concocted by Carlos was shifting their business to Burlington, Vermont, and it was perfect. Who would ever suspect a priest, especially one who had the plastic surgery to make the transition complete.

Father Frank Figuora is brought back to the present with the sound of the rectory side door closing. Glancing over, in walks Upton, a man of few words. "We need to talk."

Father Figuora speaks softly to him so no one else can hear. "Be patient, Upton." Then speaking louder for the benefit of Mrs. O'Brien,

"Can I interest you in some breakfast as I finish mine, detective? Mrs. O'Brien, please get our friend, Detective Upton, a cup of coffee. Can we get you anything else?"

"No, thank you, that will do."

Father Figuora continues with the small talk, finishing his breakfast and thanking Mrs. O'Brien for going that extra mile yet again. "Come, Charles, let's go to my office."

As Father Figuora sits down behind his desk, Upton throws Amy's cell phone at him. Figuora catches it in one hand, never taking his eyes off of him. "Who had it?"

"Youngblood. He gave it to me this morning, said he found it on the front seat of his truck."

Father Figuora nods in Upton's direction. "You believe him?" Upton shrugs.

Figuora plugs in the cell phone, surprised to see it has a charge. His eyes glued to the screen. He mutters, "He did."

Upton doesn't understand what he's referring to. "He did what?"

"Skunk called someone down in Sonora. He spent time down there, and he had this girlfriend."

Upton slides forward to the edge of his chair. "Can it come back to us?"

"To me it can. I call down there all the time, but this girl, she's a hooker. Skunk did drugs with her. Carlos will deal with her."

Upton exhales deeply. "I feel better."

"What's happening with Amy's friends?"

"The girl doesn't stay in her apartment anymore. I believe she is staying with that guy Alexander Acof at his parent's home." Father Figuora sits back in his leather desk chair, his fingers interlaced in front of his chest.

"He's been watching us you know."

"Alexander?"

"Yes. I've seen his truck up the street now and then. In fact, it was there less than thirty minutes ago."

Upton feels his heart rate increase. "No one is speculating on anything at the precinct. The only one who might know something is Youngblood. I wonder if he knows about Alexander and his surveillance?"

"So the reality is we need to be concerned about Leslie, Alexander, and Harold. Those three can bring us down."

Upton walks over to close the office door. He is feeling uneasy about the direction their conversation is taking and concerned about who may be within earshot. "I don't know what you're thinking, but we can't be taking the three of them out. Too many questions will be asked, and everything will get a lot more complicated than it feels like now."

Father Figuora nods his head in agreement silently thinking for a few minutes.

"For some reason, I believe Alexander knows more than we think. I mean, think about it, Skunk had this cell phone. How in God's name did it get out of here?"

"Frank, you're making too much out of this. I would know if Youngblood had other information. You are not killing them or having them killed."

"Listen, Charles, you're paid to keep quiet and paid quite well. If anyone finds out how Skunk actually met his demise, you'll be out of the shadows and into the light. You realize what they do to cops in prison don't you?"

Upton flops on the leather couch by the front window. Under his weight, the couch sounds like it has a gastric problem. Both men remain lost in their thoughts, thinking about how everything will play out. Figuora comes over and sits by him.

"What do we do, Charles?"

"The girl, she's not talking to anyone. I'll go through Youngblood's files to make sure of what he knows, and as far as Alexander goes, I think we should send the boys to rough him up a bit."

"And you think that'll stop him?"

Upton grins. "I've seen it hundreds of times. Guys talk big until someone physically puts a hurt on them. Then they turn into a clam."

Figuora and Upton sit, looking at each other. "What if Youngblood has something. Maybe he's getting information from the two kids."

Upton is quick to respond. "No, it would never happen. Alexander and the girl cannot be in with Youngblood."

"How can you be so sure?"

"I grant you, Youngblood is a pain in the ass but, he's a fuckin boy scout. He would never draw any civilian into a case. He is too much by the book, so if Alexander is snooping, he's on his own."

"Okay, Charles. Here's what we need, a body. We'll frame this person for Amy's murder, simple. But in the meantime, you check on Youngblood's files, and I'll make arrangements for the boys to rough up Alexander."

Upton is anxious to leave before anyone from the precinct misses him. "I think I've got just the guy we can frame and as far as Alexander goes, he needs this tune-up."

"Good. While you're at it, get something out of Amy's apartment that we can tie to the killer in case we need it. Get something from Leslie's place too. Since she hasn't been staying there, it's perfect, plus she'll never realize something is missing."

Upton leaves. "No problem."

"You give them Amy's murderer and that should be the end of it. But if it's not, I'll bring in some people who can take care of things and tie up all the loose ends. We're making too much money for our operation to stop."

14

Alexander wakes up early having promised his dad he would check on a job site that's getting behind schedule. He doesn't wake Leslie and leaves without saying good-bye. He's happy to see she is finally getting some semblance of a good night's sleep.

He can tell Leslie is feeling comfortable in his parents' home, and for the past few days, his mom joined her at the studio. She too has a flair for decorating and designing. Their home is a testament to her talent.

He grabs his laundry bag filled with dirty work clothes as he heads out and plans to stop by the studio later for coffee.

While at the same time, across town, Youngblood pulls up to a crime scene reported as a shooting. He parks next to Upton's cruiser, surprised by Charles being on the scene. He wonders how he got there before him.

Speaking of the devil, Charles exits the building and walks in his direction. "Harold, what are you doing here?"

"Heard it over the radio, thought I might be of help."

"I'm sure you did."

"So what do we have?"

"Some guy shot late last night, being the first on the scene, it looks to me like he is involved in the Peter's killing."

Upton scans his face, looking for a reaction to this news. He's disappointed when Youngblood shows no clue to what he might be thinking. "When I got here, there was no answer and the door was unlocked. I called it in, but I got tired of waiting for backup, so I went in and there he was. Dead, one shot to the head."

Every fiber in Youngblood's body came alive. This crime scene didn't feel right to him.

"Is there proof that links him to the Peter's case?"

"I'll let you know once I finish up. That Nova parked over there is registered to the victim. Here are the keys. Go check it out."

Youngblood grabs the keys and heads toward the car. Upton is feeling proud of himself. He can hardly wait until Harold finds the things from Amy's apartment in the trunk. This is better than he hoped. Smug, he returns to his crime scene.

Over at the Design Studio, Leslie and Olga with Princess and Queen, pull into the parking lot. Olga loves her new routine. "I guess we can finish up the job at the Darringtons today. We need Russell to finish hanging the curtain rods."

"Yes, we can finish up today. I'm grateful for your help with this job, Olga. You have a real talent for this work. You know, I could use your help on a regular basis, and you could earn a little money at the same time. What do you think?"

Olga is touched by her offer. "I would love that, and I would do the work for free!"

They enter the studio, and Olga gets right to work ironing the curtains before Russell loads them into the van.

Alexander couldn't break away from the job site as he initially planned. He spent the morning solving problems. He wasn't one to sit behind a desk; he preferred to work alongside the men in the dirt and the grime. His work ethic is good for the men he works alongside with; they respond to him and respect him.

Alexander accomplishes what his father asked him to do, and the project is back on schedule. He is relieved to have this assignment finished as he does not enjoy this type of work. He would rather be working on his own projects, but family comes first.

While driving back to Burlington, Al notices the white Tahoe he's seen at the rectory following him. It might have been there earlier that morning too, but a phone call distracted him. He decides to turn off the main road to see what happens.

It doesn't take long to confirm. Alexander is curious why the boys are following him. He decides to stop for lunch at the Coach Tavern just outside Burlington. Pulling his truck up in front of the bar, he scans the inside of the cab, searching for something to take with him. He needs to even up the odds in the event his suspicions are correct. Dumping the contents of his laundry bag onto the floor, he stuffs the mesh bag into his pocket. Alexander looks through the pile of work clothes, but there is nothing else worthwhile to take.

He enters the Coach Tavern where the bar is built like a big square horseshoe. It is sixty feet long with two ten-foot sections on either end. The only difference on the section where Alexander sits is it contains a flip-up panel to let the bartender in and out.

Walking toward the far end of the bar, he sees the Tahoe pass. Alexander orders a beer. He is not unfamiliar with the Coach Tavern where he occasionally shoots pool. There are four pool tables behind him. Pulling the mesh laundry bag from his pocket, Alexander grabs six billiard balls, placing them inside. He ties a knot and sets the bag down on the bar next to the wall, stretching it out to lie flat with the knot hanging down. He takes a few steps back to the corner stool, sits, and sips his beer.

He has a good view of everything from this spot. There is the bartender, two older gentlemen, and the Tahoe parked across the street with the three football players heading toward the bar. Alexander wasn't sure whether or not their size had registered accurately with him before today, but they are big boys, Leon, Brad, but especially Rock.

They enter the bar laughing and pushing each other. The bartender tells them to calm down, and they sit midbar. They order cokes and hamburgers. Leon is first to chime in, "She's a bitch."

Brad is next to take the bait. "You mean that girl who owns the design studio?"

"Yea, that's her."

This is Rock's queue. "Hey, aren't you her boyfriend?"

Alexander glances over but doesn't answer. He just sips his beer.

Rock pushes his stool back, stands, and calls out loudly, "Hey, buddy, I'm talking to you."

Leon places his hand on Rock's shoulder. "Easy, Rock, I'll take it from here. I'm the one who thinks she's a bitch, right?" Alexander thinks he's in good shape dealing with Leon first since he's not as big as Rock. Alexander smiles as Leon approaches him.

"Is there something wrong with you?"

"You talking to me?"

"Yea, I am. You know I am, and you heard me say your girl is a bitch, isn't that true?

This time Alexander gives him a big toothy grin. "I'm gonna bust your head."

All three boys get up and movie in his direction. Alexander backs up, but he's still about eight feet from the wall as Leon turns the corner. Rock is right behind him. "You got nowhere to go, big man."

Alexander is not completely out of contact range when Leon throws the first punch, a right directly at Alexander's head. He blocks his swing with his left forearm. It's a glancing blow off his shoulder. Leon is off balance from the momentum, and Alexander uses the opportunity to nail him with a right like a hammer. He sees Leon's knees buckle, and he's down on the floor dazed.

Alexander is working his way backward to the wall where his laundry bag is on the bar, but he'll need to cover another three to four feet. That means he needs to take one more hit from Leon, which lands on his jaw. Rock and Brad are stationary at the corner of the bar. Leon is rattled and his blow has nothing in it. Leslie's hit him harder. Alexander pretends he's been hit like a ton of bricks, and he backs up against the wall.

Leon comes at him again stumbling. When he's within striking distance, Alexander springs in his direction, using his arms and legs, and he thrusts his palm into Leon's chin. He can feel teeth, perhaps even his jaw, shatter as Leon goes airborne, landing on a pool table.

Rock watches in disbelief as his friend rolls on the pool table, and he heads in for the kill. Alexander grabs the end of the laundry bag, making it taut, and whips it off the bar with just enough time for one circle over his head to gather force and slams the bag into the side of the Rock's head. He is thrust back, cartwheeling over the pool table and hitting the pool light with his feet. Light beams shoot back and forth across the room as the balls break free from the laundry bag, rocketing toward Brad, who throws his arms up to protect his head. Alexander moves in right behind them. His fists find their mark, bouncing Brad to the wall, hitting the back of his head and knocking a Coors Light sign to the floor.

Everything happened so fast, the bartender is only now next to Alexander. "Are you all right?"

"Yes,"

"These boys are always trouble. I called the police." Alexander stuffs the laundry bag into his pocket and returns to his stool, sits down, and sips his beer.

"You hungry?"

"Yes, actually I am," Alexander replies. The bartender slides over one of the hamburgers in front of him. He smiles at Alexander and says, "It's on them." He picks up the cash and puts it in the register. Alexander thanks him for the burger and offers to pay for the damages.

Across town, Upton hears the call come in over the radio and drives over to the Coach Tavern. There is another patrol car and an ambulance there when he arrives. As he walks over to the bar, he's whistling a mindless tune. He is feeling quite satisfied with himself and sighs how he loves when a plan comes together. He walks through the tavern door, and what he sees changes his mood. There is Alexander at the bar eating a burger.

Upton takes in the entire scene and blurts out, "You've done it now, Alexander."

But before he can get out another word, the bartender cuts him off, "Leave him alone. He was protecting himself." With that the two other patrons agree. Upton is dumbfounded. He grabs the arm of the patrolman. "Is that right?"

"Yes, sir, that's how it went down."

Upton can't understand how this went wrong, but even more worrisome is how will Figuora take it?

15

Alexander is allowed to leave the Coach Tavern around four o'clock. He's tired, mentally and physically. He thinks he should just go home, get in a hot tub, and perhaps take a nap before dinner. Once he's inside his truck driving, he feels a bit better and thinks he might stop by the design studio since it appears he's getting a second wind.

He called Leslie earlier to let her know what happened. He did not want her to worry.

Pulling up to the studio, he spots Leslie's car and the studio van parked in front. He made up his mind to stop. As he walks past the front window, there lay Queen and Princess, taking advantage of the sunlight while resting on a beautiful oriental rug. Their heads keep pace with his approach.

Opening the front door, the buzzer goes off. From the back, Leslie calls out that she will be right out. Alexander knows his mom is here since Queen is here. He looks around the studio, noticing the new video cameras recently installed. His eyes go up to the front of the studio. The three wing chairs and coffee table have a new addition, a two-drawer file cabinet. He walks to the wing chair and flops down, exhaling deeply. His second wind was short lived. He begins to think he may not leave here tonight, especially if he had an ottoman. Leslie comes out of the back room spotting him.

Leslie's pace quickens, and he sees his mom is not too far behind her. "Are you all right?"

"Yes, I'm fine."

His mom studies his injuries. "Those men, did they hurt you?"

"They were just boys, mom. I'm really fine. I'm just tired."

Leslie sits down in the chair next to him while his mom replies, "From what we were told, they were big boys."

Alexander looks at Leslie, confused. "Youngblood was here not too long ago. In fact, he just left. One of the patrolmen filled Youngblood in on what happened, and he told us you were all right. He told him you were attacked. Did you know them, Alexander?"

"Would it surprise you to learn it was the three football players?"

Leslie is not really surprised. "Actually, I'm not all that surprised with everything that's happening. Youngblood said he doesn't want Upton to know he was here. He thinks the less Upton knows about us, the better, but he wanted to fill us in. He also said you really pissed off Upton."

"I'm glad he came by. It's good to know people are looking out for us." He turned his attention to his mom. "Did you call dad?"

"I did. It is important for him to know, Alexander. Hey, I picked up a chocolate cheesecake for tonight. We can sprinkle some confectionary sugar and whipped cream on it with some fresh cherries tonight."

Leslie turns her attention to Olga. She can't believe this conversation. Leslie loved cheesecake as much as the next person, but her son had been beaten up and here she is talking cake.

Alexander wants to laugh at her reaction. His mom, hardened from all those years in Russia, made her strong. Alexander really loved her.

He smiles his biggest smile at her. "That sounds great!"

Leslie shakes her head in disbelief. "If the two of you were on the Titanic, you would have been in deck chairs listening to the quartet play."

Upton drove over to the rectory. He's there to talk with Figuora about bringing in professionals. He is against it. They were in a good place. They had a killer tied to the Amy Peters killing; that should appease everyone. He enters the rectory feeling confident he can control Figuora. He cannot let this get out of hand.

As Upton enters the rectory through the front door, he spots Figuora in his office behind his desk. Upton takes in a deep breath and goes inside.

Father Figuora didn't know anything yet. "Charles, I was just thinking about you. How did things go?"

"First off, the good news is it seems everyone is buying this plant as Amy Peters' murderer. Even Youngblood helped confirm this, and if Mr. By the Book believes, everyone else will easily buy in. And I went through Youngblood's files. There is absolutely nothing on this case that we need to be concerned about. Plus moving forward, anything that comes in on this case goes through me and me only."

"Good, good. So far we're heading in the right direction but I have not heard from the boys yet."

"And you most likely won't for a while." This has his full attention. "Why is that?"

"The bad news is Alexander managed to turn the tables on them, and the boys were beaten pretty bad."

"How is that possible? Did he have help?"

"Not that I saw. The tavern only had the bartender and two other patrons. One of whom walks with a cane."

"I can't believe that. The boys are so strong. Alexander had to have help."

"I was just as surprised but Alexander handled them all on his own."

"So what's the plan now, Charles?"

"We let it ride. We see what happens now that the killer's been found. This should stop everyone from looking any further, and the fight in the tavern just looks like a fight in a tavern ignited by bar talk."

Father Figuora sits looking out the front window. "I hope you're right, Charles; but remember, if anything else happens, I step in to take care of things my way."

It is coming close to 7:00 p.m., and Alexander is sleeping in the wing chair. His mother watches him sleep.

"Olga, why don't you take my car and both dogs, and we'll meet you at the house?"

"Sounds good, dear. I'll go make dinner. Lock the door behind us."

Leslie lets Olga out of the studio, locks the door, and watches her get into the car and drive off. She walks over by Alexander and gives him a gentle nudge to wake him up.

He stretches and yawns. "I think I need to take this chair home with me."

"It's yours. We need to get going, Alexander. Your mom is expecting us for dinner."

"Not tonight, Leslie. Do you mind? I would rather go out for Italian food. I'll call her and tell her."

"Well, far be it from me to pass up Italian food."

The roads are packed with traffic when they left the studio. Alexander gets on Route 89 North, heading to Saint Albans, hoping to get there quicker. They had not talked about what happened to him this afternoon. This is the perfect time for that conversation.

"Alexander, were you scared?"

"I would be lying if I said I wasn't. I'm more concerned about why it happened."

"Youngblood also mentioned they found Amy's murderer, and although it seems hinky, he wants us to act like we believe it's true. Youngblood is convinced Father Figuora is somehow involved, and that finding the murderer was staged for everyone's benefit."

Alexander parks the truck, and they enter the restaurant, sitting at their favorite table as the waitress comes over smiling. They order their usual, and the waitress leaves to put in the order and get their drinks.

Alexander looks into Leslie's face. "I need to get back into that rectory."

From her body language, it is clear Leslie disagrees; but before she can voice her obvious objections, Alexander continues, "Just listen to me first then tell me what you think. With the killer supposedly found, the police will have no more interest in Figuora, and things will go back to usual."

"That's not true, Al. Youngblood is convinced that Father Figuora is involved. He's even said there's more there than what meets the eye, plus we promised we'd stay away."

"Face it, Leslie, there is only so much Youngblood can and will do. His hands are tied to a degree. Skunk is Figuora's man, and his involvement in all this has yet to be uncovered. Figuora needs to pay for what he's done, and right now, we're unsure exactly what that is. If we don't do something, nothing will get done. I want the real person who killed Amy, and we need to know why."

"Well, you're not going into the rectory. Not only did we promise Youngblood, but Figuora and the boys know who you are now, so we need to figure out something else."

Silently they eat dinner. Alexander is tired, but his mind is racing, trying to figure out what their next move should be. He needs to get to Figuora.

16

Alexander stays in bed the next morning. He doesn't feel up to going to work today, besides he is feeling sore from yesterday's encounter with the boys.

He continues to feel as he did last night, about needing to do something. Figuora and all the people responsible for Amy's death need to be held accountable. He hears a knock on his door; it is Leslie.

"Can I come in?"

"Sure, I'm awake. Come on in." Leslie opens the door wide, and Princess comes bounding in, jumps up on the bed to kiss Alexander. She is happy to see him.

"I'm not moving real well today, so I'm going to take the day off plus I have some things to take care of."

"Your mom and dad thought you might need rest today. I'm going to the studio. Your mom and the dogs will be with me. Feel better, Alexander. I'll see you back here tonight."

Alexander waits until the house is quiet to get out of bed and dress. He goes down for breakfast, and walking into the kitchen, there sits Karl and Carl.

"Carl, watch out. There are only two of us here, and we're no match for him," Karl teased.

Alexander laughs. "That's the most you've said to me in two years. I didn't even think you two speak English!"

"Had nothing to talk about till now. You know, if this priest is involved in moving drugs, you can bring down some real problems on all of us."

His brother chimes in, "I hope so. I need some excitement."

Alexander is nervous. "I'm worried about mom and Leslie."

"Alexander, we know you're going to do what you must, but if you push this right, there is going to be ramifications."

"I know, but I just can't sit still and let this go. This priest is dirty."

"Do what you must. The dogs will not let anyone near your mom and Leslie. Let us know so we can keep an eye on what's going on."

Carl chimes in, "Count me in."

Alexander feels good at their offering help. "I don't know what I'm going to do yet. How's my dad?"

"He knows you. Why do you think we're here waiting to talk? He's asked us to be alert, and we wanted to make sure you knew."

"I'm going to take a ride. I need to think."

"I thought your thinking place is up by the lake?"

"This is a driving problem."

Alexander grabs a bandana on his way out the door, gets into his truck, and heads for town. He's decided if he can't go to the rectory, there is nothing stopping him from going to the bus terminal. He pulls into the parking lot across the street from the terminal and watches as people come and go. Alexander is restless, uncertain about what to do from here, so he decides to go inside.

As he walks through the glass doors, he heads for the men's room passing a bank of lockers. He notices the key is in locker number eleven, and then the idea hits him. He turns back, puts money in the locker, removes the key, and heads back toward his truck. He thinks John the pawnbroker might be able to duplicate the key.

Alexander drives to the pawnshop. John is also a licensed locksmith. He knows locker keys are special, but he feels that if anyone can duplicate the key, John will be the man.

Not far from this location, Upton decides to check on Father Figuora to make sure nothing has changed. He is concerned he may decide to bring in outsiders. This will lead to big trouble for him if people start getting killed around town.

He pulls his cruiser into the parking lot of the rectory, entering the side entrance through the kitchen. Mrs. O'Brien is baking apple pies. Upton tries to steal an apple, but Mrs. O'Brien slaps his hand away; and he continues moving into the hallway, approaching Figuora's office. He hears voices as he walks in.

"Charles, I want you to meet Father Clarkson and Father Payne. The diocese has sent them to monitor the progress we're making with the poor and homeless in this area."

Charles realizes he's too late for his intended conversation, which is confirmed by the look on Figuora's face and his introduction. These aren't real priests. They show no emotion, are in exceptionally good shape, and do not express a need to know who he is. He knows his nightmare has come true. He decides to play along.

"Pleased to meet you. How long will you be in town?"

Neither of them replies but Figuora does. "Not too long, Charles."

He turns to his guests to let them know Mrs. O'Brien will show them to their rooms. He buzzes Mrs. O'Brien and hands them off to her.

"I thought you were going to wait?'

"They're just here as insurance, and if I need to do something, I can jump right on it. So, Charles, it's up to you to see nothing gets to that point. I hope you're up for the job."

Alexander makes the turn into John's lot. It is filled by several cars, and Alexander finds a space. He feels eager to talk with John, but based on the parking lot, he will most likely have to be patient.

Alexander is correct. Once John notices Alexander pacing back and forth, he wraps up his deal by doing a friendly handoff to one of his salespeople to finish the transaction. John walks over to where Alexander is wearing a path in his carpet. "Alexander, what's up? You appear anxious. Is everything okay?"

"Hi, John, sorry. I need something and it may or may not be considered honest."

"By the look on your face, I think I can answer that for you. Why don't you just ask me and let me be the judge? I know you're facing something challenging even if I don't have all the details. Plus your dad called me and asked me to give you whatever you need. So what is it you need?"

Alexander shakes his head in disbelief and feels much better than when he walked into the store. "My dad is always one step ahead of me."

John places his hand on Alexander's shoulder, leading him further into the store so they can have more privacy. "Your dad knows lots of things. He knows how to run a business, that's for sure. He knows how to size up people. That's something most CEOs don't get. He's a good judge of character, which helps him decide where to place his loyalties."

"What do you think he'd say if he knew I wanted a duplicate of this?" With that, Alexander pulls the terminal locker key from his pocket and shows it to him in his open hand.

John takes the key from him to examine it closer. "Duplicating this could get me into trouble. Come with me."

"You're not going to ask me any questions, John?"

"I don't have a need to know. Your father will call me to find out what you needed, and I will tell him."

John brings Alexander to his workbench to fabricate a second key for him. It only takes a few minutes. He turns off the equipment and bathed in the overhead light then hands both keys back to Alexander.

"If this goes bad, you don't know me and I don't know you."

Alexander understands, feeling grateful for his help. "Don't worry, John, you're safe with me. What do I owe you?"

"I'll take that up with your dad."

"Thank you, John."

Alexander leaves the shop. The plan is to drive back to the bus terminal and replace the key in locker 11 before anyone notices it missing. Before pulling out, he calls Bert, asking him to stake out the bus terminal, watch locker 11, and call him when something is placed inside. Then wait for him to arrive and let him know if anyone pulled out what's inside before he gets there.

He's going to retrieve the contents of the locker while Bert sticks around to make sure he is not followed.

Bert's response is just what Alexander wants to hear. "You've got it, Alexander. I'm on my way there now."

Alexander isn't sure if Bert is joking, but when he gets there, he spots him reading a newspaper over by the soda machine. Alexander replaces the key. Everything is set, and it's time to go talk with his father.

As he pulls through the front gate, he sees his father's Hummer at the carriage house. He reaches for the side door as Carl opens it.

"Alexander."

"Hi, Carl, is my dad here?"

"Yup. He's downstairs in the basement."

Alexander's heartbeat picks up. He proceeds downstairs, wondering what's going on. He finds his dad and Karl next to a four-by-eight-foot plywood table. There on top are two AK-47s, four Glock 9mm handguns with shoulder holsters, and four blades in sheathes.

Alexander asks his father, "What's going on?"

Urie's eyes never leave the gun he's inspecting. "We're getting ready for trouble. It's time to prepare."

"It's not going to go that far, Dad. At least it hasn't gotten there yet."

"Alexander, you don't wait until trouble happens. You prepare yourself for it. I've always taught you the best defense is offense, and the events warn us to be prepared for whatever may come."

"Yes, Dad, I agree but this?" Alexander sweeps his hand through the air, indicating the table's contents.

"Yes, my son. The AK-47s are for Carl and Karl to use around the property. We're out here alone, and we need to be prudent. I have a handgun and a knife for you too."

"Dad, I'm not..."

But before he can go any further, Urie cuts off his objection. "Yes, you will or you're going to stop whatever it is you're working on right now. So make your decision and call Bert."

Karl, the man of few words, says, "Your father knows best, Alexander. One good thing, the weather is cold enough, so concealing your weapon will be easy to do under your jacket."

"Okay, you win. I'll do it." Alexander knows in his heart this is the best approach. His dad would never place his life or anyone else in the family in danger.

Urie turns to face everyone. "Remember, these are for protection. I spoke with John earlier; we could find ourselves in some trouble."

Karl picks up his weapons and asks Urie if there is anything else. Urie instructs him to pull out night vision goggles for him and his brother. Once accomplished, both brothers get ready to leave the carriage house. Before they exit, Alexander hugs them both. He can tell they are uncomfortable with his display of affection, and without saying a word, they quickly leave.

Alexander is alone with his father. "Dad, I hope you understand I need to do this. That priest is the reason Amy is dead, and that episode at the tavern tells me I'm already in trouble, and I'm getting close to whatever they do not want me to know."

"That's part of the reason we're taking these precautions, son. Just keep me in the loop on what you're doing and when, Alexander."

With that Alexander hugs his dad. He walks across the property back to the main house. He knows the main gate will be locked from now on, forcing visitors and family to enter past the carriage house. As Alexander enters the kitchen, he is happy to see Leslie and his mom both there.

"Hmm, something smells good. What is it?'

Laughing, Olga grins at their son. "We picked up Chinese food!"

17

After dinner, everyone sits in the living room talking. Urie builds a fire. Leslie feels like family as she sits on the couch next to Alexander with her feet up to the side, leaning on the armrest, sipping hot chocolate. The past two weeks brought her closer to them, and they've helped her with the loss of her friend, at least initially. Leslie understands she will never completely get over her loss. All she knows right now is that this arrangement makes her feel good.

Olga, sipping her hot chocolate, said, "I love hot chocolate before bed."

Leslie has to chime in, "I agree! It's a great way to end the day."

Olga shifts her focus to her husband. "Urie, did you get to talk with Alexander today?"

"I did, honey. Everything is all set."

Leslie's in the dark about what they're referring to. If Urie wants her to know, he will tell her, but right now it looks like he did not. She waits to see if any further information is forthcoming but then curiosity gets the better of her.

"What's all set?"

Alexander does not have a chance to answer before his dad takes the lead.

"We feel it's time to take precautions against the priest. Through no fault of anyone, we've been dragged into a situation, which we don't know a lot about nor how it will end up, so the best thing we can do is prepare."

"Shouldn't the police be involved?"

"They are, through Sergeant Youngblood, but he's only one man and now that a body's been produced that supposedly ties into Amy's murder, the smart thing to do is get prepared."

"Who are you, people? You act as if Alexander is riding without a helmet!" Sorrow fills her face. She misses Amy, the girl who loved life, challenged it to accept her on her terms and not life's terms. She's sad that this wonderful family is part of her problem through no fault of their own. Olga comes over, sits down, and puts her arms around her.

"I'm sorry, dear. No one here is to blame, but we need to talk about it. Because of that body, the police closed their case. That's why we need to set rules and make sure everyone is cautious. Just the fact they came after my son tells us they're uncertain of what he knows and makes us guilty by association."

"I know it's true. I just worry something bad can happen to anyone or all of us."

Urie joins them on the couch. "You're right, dear, but what better way to control this situation?"

Leslie is overwhelmed. "Mr. and Mrs. Acof, you're wonderful parents and so different than what I'm used to. You have more trust in your son than most parents."

"My son is no different than how we feel about you, Leslie. He is a hard worker in everything he does, never takes days off, and he is dependable. My wife and I are upfront with him, never had the need to lie, and we always found a way to explain the whys to what we do. We built trust."

"My parents still don't talk to me because of the career choice I made, and trust in my family only goes one way, to them."

"Yes, my dear, and that's unfortunate, but I'm sure they love you. It's just in their own way, guided by their opinion of what you should do with your life."

"What would you have done if Alexander wanted to go into a different business?"

"We would have let him. A parent needs to have faith in their children. We worked to instill values in him from a young age, and with that foundation, he is set free to go in his own direction."

"You need to talk with my parents."

Urie smiles at her. "All children are different. Some need discipline or direction from their parents, and maybe this worked with your older brother and sister, so they stuck with that same approach."

Leslie hated to admit it, but it made sense.

"Let me ask you this, Leslie. If you never met Amy, would you have gone into interior design or would you have followed your parents' suggestions?"

"I hate to admit this, but I would have followed their advice."

Leslie felt honored and lucky to have known Amy. Her eyes tear up, and Olga hugs her. She announces, "Enough of this talk. We need cheesecake. We never ate any last night."

Leslie perks up. "Sounds good to me right now."

"Good. I'll get everything ready and, Urie, can you put on a pot of coffee?"

As his parents leave the room, Alexander slides closer to Leslie and puts his arm around her.

"They mean well."

"You have no idea how lucky you are. Hell, they're great."

Alexander is surprised by her using a swear word. He's never heard her do that in the four years they've known each other. "Well, let's go into the kitchen, Miss Potty Mouth."

18

The next morning, the breakfast conversation is lively, filled with making plans and identifying things that need to be completed that day. Alexander is the last one to join the group in the kitchen. He walks in and grabs a cup of coffee.

"Good morning all."

"It's about time you decided to join us, Al. You missed another delicious breakfast, but cook put some in the oven for you."

Alexander retrieves his breakfast and sits down at the table. His dad is dunking three-day-old donuts in his coffee cup and is buried in the newspaper while, across the table, the girls finish up their planning. Leslie and his mom stand to leave for the studio. Leslie comes over to kiss him. With well wishes for a good day and a promise to see him later, they grab their bags.

"Come, Queen. Come, Princess." And with that being said, they're gone. The cook follows after them while Karl and Carl push their way out the door. Alexander's dad shrugs his shoulders and stands, announcing he has things to do; leaving the room, he heads in the other direction. King and Duke follow him.

Alexander eats alone. Once done, he walks over to the carriage house where he left his truck last night. Karl is standing outside.

"Good morning, Karl."

"Morning, Alexander. The main gate is going to be locked until further notice, so you'll need to come in past the carriage house from now on." Karl pulls Alexander's jacket open to check on whether or not he had the Glock. He does.

Alexander is curious about why Karl likes an AK-47 and asks him about it. "I think it's one of the best assault rifles out there. You can drop it in water, sand, mud, and a jeep can drive over it, and it still fires. I like it because it's dependable."

"Just like you, Karl."

Alexander leaves, dialing Bert's number.

"Morning, Bert. How did last night go?"

"I stayed until midnight, and I got back here at 6:00 a.m. I'm positioned west of the terminal. All the glass gives me a good view, and I have the locker in sight. I need to try something different instead of sitting in the terminal all day."

"Sounds good. Call me if you need a break."

Alexander drives over to the job site. Today it is on a pier with a two-story boathouse. The lower portion is designed for the customer to dock their boat. Today they will install a lift cradle to take the boat out of the water and into the lower level. The boat is secured, and the floorboards moved back into place. Once they close, a locking mechanism activates, securing the floor. A limit switch automatically shuts down the left motor.

This is the type of job Alexander likes to work on in addition to his love for woodworking. As he pulls down the driveway toward the boathouse, Sergeant Youngblood is right behind him. Parking, Youngblood pulls alongside his truck.

"Good morning, sergeant."

"Good morning, Alexander. You keeping clear of the rectory?"

"Yes, sir, I am. My dad told me the police closed Amy's case. Is that true?"

"It's true, Alexander. That supposed murderer Upton found clinched it."

"Unbelievable. Does that bother you? I mean we know Skunk did it. So this means not only did someone kill Skunk, but someone committed another murder too. Tell me that bothers you."

Youngblood just looks straight ahead and does not answer him. His eyes take in the construction site.

"What's on the second floor?"

"It's an apartment. Do you plan on answering me?"

"Let's look at what we know. We have a murderer in town, and this murderer has killed two homeless people. It's not much of a stretch to include a store owner and her boyfriend. That's why I asked you to stay clear of the rectory and take precautions."

Alexander buttons his jacket. He wasn't sure if Youngblood suspects he's carrying a gun, or maybe it's just his statement about taking precautions.

"So what you're not saying is Figuora is protected, and there is no reason to investigate any further."

"Not exactly. I'm saying if this drug-running thing is true, we will get Figuora. I probably should not say this to you, but my gut tells me Upton is in this too somehow. I need to catch him red-handed. Alexander, if I were to go to the captain with the limited information we have now, I wouldn't get an arrest on anyone. The only thing I'd do is put you and Leslie out there in harm's way."

Other vehicles begin pulling in, and as the men got out, they slowly make their way toward Alexander.

"Don't leave yet, sergeant. I need time to talk with you."

Alexander unlocks the tool box on his truck, and everyone grabs something then heads toward the boathouse.

"Do you think you waited too long without letting the captain know what you suspect is going on?"

"I am trying to protect you and Leslie. I have nothing concrete on Father Figuora yet. The only thing I got from the Catholic diocese is his picture, some minor information, and the picture matches. As far as Upton goes, I've got nothing concrete on him either even though there have been rumors about him for years."

"Isn't the fact we found Amy's cell phone at the rectory something?"

"It's no smoking gun, Alexander. If it ties Skunk in, that's great but he's dead. Figuora helps the homeless, but more often than not, the homeless are painted with having mental problems, so we can't tie Figuora to anything using that."

"Great. I gotta go to work."

Over at the studio, Olga and Leslie prepare items needed for their next job. Leslie is up front, calling out the items off her inventory list while Olga and Kathleen gather them and place them in a box. The door sensor beeps, and Leslie looks up from her paperwork to see Father Figuora.

Father Figuora nods to Mrs. Acof. That little gesture sets off Queen and Princess. They're growling at him and slowly moving forward to the edge of the display window, eyes locked on him. Olga walks over, and standing in front of the dogs, gives them the command to stop. They instantly do as instructed, their tails wagging at her with each one taking a position next to her. This gives Leslie a feeling of strength.

Figuora is visibly shaken. The dogs catch him off guard, gluing him to his spot. When he finally gathers his wits about him he looks toward Leslie asking her if she is all right. She thanks him and assures him she's worked through her problems.

Figuora just stands there looking at Leslie, unsure about whether or not he dare approach her. Leslie reads his mind but doesn't come to his rescue. As far as she's concerned, he can just stand there.

Leslie breaks the silence. "Father, whenever I have trouble, I turn to God, my parents, and Alexander's parents. With their collective help, I'm able to work things out. Do you still go to your parents when you need to talk, Father?"

"No, dear, my parents are deceased."

Figuora does not realize it, but he walked right into Leslie's trap. She is seeing if he'll talk about his mom in California.

"How long have they been gone?"

"Over ten years now. Both of them were killed in a car crash."

"I'm sorry to hear that."

"Well, since you're okay, I'm going to head out. If you need anything, come see me at the rectory, dear." With that he turns and quickly leaves. His exit is awkward as he backs out. Leslie is thrilled he is afraid of dogs. She can't stomach it when he calls her dear.

At 11:30 a.m., Alexander's cell phone goes off. He looks at the display: it's Bert.

"Yea, Bert."

"I need to get some lunch, use the head, and stretch my legs."

"I'll be right over."

Alexander instructs his foreman to let the men take an early lunch, and they talk through what to start with after lunch. He lets him know he will be back as soon as possible.

Alexander and Bert exchange roles. Everything is quiet at the bus terminal, so once Bert returns, Alexander heads back to the job. He wonders if their routine changed, and perhaps they just aren't aware of that yet. They'll find out.

Sergeant Youngblood is back at the precinct. The paperwork portion of his job is his least favorite thing, but it provides the perfect cover for keeping an eye on Upton. It seems to Youngblood, Charles is acting anxious the past several days. His plan is to work his way into his confidence even if it kills him, and he thinks it probably will.

"Charles."

"Yea, Harold."

Well, that is something unusual, Charles as a nice guy, Youngblood muses to himself as he makes a mental note of the date and time. "You did a good job on the Peters' case, Charles. Is there anything else I can help you with?"

"Thanks, Harold, but I have nothing else I need help with right now."

"Okay. If anything comes up, call me." Youngblood cannot explain why but he has a moment of feeling sorry for the big ape.

Back at the boathouse job site, the work is progressing well, and it's now 3:00 p.m. The first level of the boathouse is complete. It has the best workshop that anyone would envy, complete with a radial arm saw and countertops on either side. It creates an area where you can easily cut or rip wood in either direction with cabinets both overhead and below.

Around 4:00 p.m., Alexander's cell phone rings. It's Bert.

"The drops been made."

"Okay, I'm on my way."

19

Alexander is fired up and double-parks in front of the bus terminal. Without thinking twice, he heads right for locker 11, key in hand. Opening the locker, he grabs the duffle bag and returns to his truck. He looks straight ahead seeing no one, not even Bert.

A few miles down the road his cell phone goes off and Alexander answers using his Bluetooth. "Yea."

"No one followed you, Al. I'm off duty, amigo. I'm tired and hungry. We'll catch up tomorrow."

"Good. Thanks, Bert. You did a great job, and I appreciate it."

Alexander turns his truck around, heading for home, which is in the opposite direction. He drove in this direction when he left the bus terminal in the event he was being followed. He didn't plan on leading anyone to his home. He's on the dirt road in a flash, and Karl waves at him to park in front of the main house. Grabbing the bag from the front seat, he heads for his father's study.

The study door is open with his father seated behind his desk.

Urie looks up. "Alexander." Alexander takes the duffle bag and tosses it on his father's desk. "The locker?"

"Yes."

Urie opens the bag. It's loaded with cash and a list in some type of code. Urie counts the money while Alexander watches.

"There is $380,000 dollars here."

"And a bag like this leaves the rectory at least once a week, sometimes more often."

"That adds up to roughly twenty mil a year."

"That we know of…"

"They're not selling all that junk here in Burlington. It's most likely being moved through here to the bigger cities."

"I don't think I can put this back because, by now, they must know it's gone."

At that moment, Alexander's mom comes home with the dogs, and she walks into the study.

"Where is Leslie, mom?"

"She is at the studio. She tried calling you to pick her up tonight."

Alexander pats his pockets. "I must have left my cell phone in the truck. I'll be back."

"Hey, son, Leslie shouldn't stay at the apartment for a while. Why not take her over there to pick up everything she will need to stay here for at least a few days."

"Will do, dad. If you ask me, I don't think she wants to leave here, and I can't blame her." Olga grins at her son. She is blessed to have raised such a good person.

Alexander runs to his truck, listens to Leslie's phone message, and calls her. "Hi, honey, sorry about missing your call. I'm on my way. Is everything okay there?"

"Yup, Sergeant Youngblood is here, and I forced a cup of tea on him." Alexander feels his pulse slow down, followed with the acceleration of his truck.

"Good. I'm on my way. Just try to keep him there, but don't say anything. Just try to keep him there."

"Okay, honey, I will."

He's unsure exactly why he told her to keep him there, but it really didn't matter. Sometimes you need to just listen to your gut. He wrestles with whether or not he should tell Youngblood what he's done.

Alexander enters the studio and finds Sergeant Youngblood sitting in his favorite wing chair.

"Hello, Alexander."

"Hello, sergeant. We never know when you're going to pop up. Did something happen?"

"Just keeping my eye on the two of you, making sure all is okay. Well, now that you're here, I'm going to take off. Good night, kids."

Alexander decides not to say anything, but as soon as Youngblood leaves, he wastes no time in giving Leslie the bum's rush to get out of there.

"Leslie, let's get everything you need from your apartment so you can stay by us for the next few days. I think you can close up a little early so we can get that done. What do you think?"

Alexander catches sight of Youngblood as he pulls out of the parking lot heading toward the precinct. He looks over at Leslie who, it is evident on her face, is totally confused.

"I'll fill you in on everything as we head to your apartment. Now go close up so we can get out of here."

Leslie lets Kathleen go home early, sets the alarm and they are off to her apartment.

Alexander is animated as he fills her in on what happened that day. His is so intent on not missing one detail, he never notices they're being followed. The apartment parking is frustrating. There is never a parking space in the front of the complex. Leslie and Alexander park around back and walk to the door.

"Parking is the one thing I will never miss about this place. I don't know how you can stand it, Leslie."

"I know. This is an older complex, and most people have more than one vehicle."

They enter Leslie's second-floor apartment, and Alexander closes the door engaging the deadbolt. Leslie hears the click of the deadbolt, confirming her suspicion that Alexander is nervous. She is about to bust him about it, but before she has a chance to, a ball breaks through the window fronting the fire escape. It hits the wood floor and slides in between them and the kitchen stove. Leslie doesn't know what it is, but it isn't a ball. Instinctively, she pushes Alexander up the hall into her bedroom. Alexander pulls her past him and closes the bedroom door.

The thermal grenade explodes a second before Alexander has the door completely closed. Flames flash around the perimeter of the doorway, but once the door securely closes, there is no danger. The door is constructed of solid wood, which helps. Alexander feels sure the results would be different if it was a hollow plastic one more commonly used today.

He quickly evaluates their best escape. "We can't get to the fire escape, so we have to find another way out. We must stay away from the windows. I have an idea." Alexander moves the bed in front of the bedroom door and walks over to the wall. He knocks on the wall, listening for the sounds that indicate the location of the wall studs. Once he gets his bearings, he punches a hole in the sheetrock. The studs are sixteen inches on center, which gives them fourteen and a half inches to slip through. Pulling out the insulation, he punches a hole in the far wall.

"Thank god this is not block construction. It's a two-by-six stick built."

Leslie is the first through followed by Alexander. They enter their neighbor's bedroom, and coming into the living room, they find her neighbors at their front door looking into the hall.

"Get out now…fire!"

"Where did you come from?"

"No time for that now. There is a fire. We need to get everyone out. Leslie, you take one side of the hall and I'll take the other."

Going from door to door, they tell everyone it's necessary to leave right now through the first floor. Once finished, Alexander grabs Leslie's arm, yelling, "Follow me."

Running through the front door of one of the first floor apartments, they cut through the dining room to the sliding glass doors. In one swift movement, they're on the patio across the lawn and jumping the back fence to the street. They sprint down three blocks to the bus stop just as it pulls to the curb. Alexander leads Leslie to the back of the bus where he remains standing to make sure they're not followed. Both of them breathing heavily, they draw attention from the people around them. Leslie notices the looks they're getting.

"That's the very last time I let you read the bus schedule."
This brings laughter to the people sitting close by.

20

Alexander, once satisfied they weren't followed, finally sits down next to Leslie. She makes light of what they just went through. Looking at him, she states in a serious tone, "I forgot to water my plants." They both laugh.

"You were good back there, Red."

"We were lucky back there," she said, shaking her head. "You really had to take that duffle bag, right Alexander?"

"I know, but I need to figure out what's going on. One thing's for sure, Figuora came back with a quick response, don't you think?"

"Somehow it feels like he was ready, like he knew it was you. Any idea on how he put all that together? Oh, and I forgot to tell you he stopped by the studio this afternoon?"

"Did he intimidate you?"

"No. The dogs took care of him by scaring the bejesus out of him. I really love those dogs. We owe them a steak dinner. I pushed the envelope a little too by asking him about his parents."

"What did you ask him? I thought only his mom was alive?"

"I was testing him, Al, and he told me they were both killed in a car crash ten years ago."

"Interesting. Here's where we get off. Come on, it's time to go."

One look around told Leslie exactly where they were headed. They're in the neighborhood of John and his pawnshop. Alexander leads them down an alley and into a fenced-in yard filled with lots of treasures. There are trucks, metal, lumber along with anything and everything imaginable. At the back of the building is a garage door housing a small access door. The only light on the building is a big floodlight above the garage door with a doorbell off to the side. Alexander rings the bell.

"John lives in the back of the pawnshop. Smile for the camera." Leslie follows his line of sight and looks into the camera. They hear a noise come from inside, and the little access door slowly opens.

John speaks in a hurried, commanding tone, "Get the hell in here! Are you in trouble?"

"You can say that. Someone tossed a thermal grenade into Leslie's apartment while we were locked inside."

John scans the surveillance cameras. It is clear by his body language he is on full alert. "This is not good. Things can get out of hand." John looks at both of them and decides to change the subject for Leslie's sake.

"Hello, Leslie, I'm glad to see you again. I got lots of new things in that you might be interested to look at. The kind of things you use to finish off a room. You know what I mean? Like the kind of stuff you get at Pier 1."

Leslie is excited at this prospect, grateful to return to thinking about something she loves and happy to push the earlier part of this evening out of her mind. "Really, John? Where are they?"

Alexander clicks his tongue and, looking at Leslie, says, "Now you're getting like my mother."

"How so might I ask?"

"Cheesecake."

"Oh my goodness!" Leslie bursts out laughing. It is as if a pressure valve released. "I can't wait to tell my parents about that, Leslie."

Anxious to see the new things John spoke about, she looks to ask him where they are but sees he is gone. "Where did John go?"

"He went that way, over there."

They head off in the direction Alexander points to and walk through a door into a beautiful kitchen. All the cabinets are cherry, and the countertops marble. There is a marble single-bowl farmhouse sink with a chiseled apron in two locations and a huge refrigerator with cherry panels. There are two stoves and an island in the center, which is four feet wide and eight feet long. The copper pots and pans hang from a suspended rack of polished stainless steel. Both oven hoods are also constructed in stainless steel, and the lighting is impeccable, leaving no area in the shadows. He has two dishwashers, and the floor is covered in twelve-inch square ceramic tiles.

John watches Leslie's face as she takes in his kitchen. He can read her approval. "I like to cook on my time off. Can I get you guys something?"

Both Alexander and Leslie answer in unison, "Coffee."

"Anyone want flavored?"

Leslie can't believe her good luck. "Do you have any raspberry coffee?"

"I do and now you will too. Good choice."

Leslie continues checking out the kitchen as John prepares the coffee. Off to the side is a cherry table eight feet long held up by four ten-inch-diameter turned legs evenly spaced. Each has a carved tiger's claw holding a ball, and there are eight ornate chairs.

John approaches the table with milk, sugar, a coffee carafe, and five mugs balanced carefully on a tray.

"I called your dad earlier. He told me you used the key tonight, and then I picked up the fire alarm on my scanner. I had a bad feeling."

Just then a buzz goes off, making John look at the property surveillance screen. As he does this, he explains the sound is triggered by the sensor signaling when anyone pulls down the driveway. He instructs Alexander to go open the garage door so his father can pull in.

Within a matter of minutes, the Hummer is inside the building, and the garage door is once again closed. The first out of the truck is his father. "Everything and everybody all right?"

"Yes."

Karl exits from the driver's side of the vehicle. When Alexander reenters the kitchen, he is amused to see his father fixing himself a cup of coffee. Urie is talking to John. "Everything went fine, John. We were not followed."

"This is a professional hit you know. They used a thermal grenade."

Leslie is feeling surreal. "What do we do now?"

Alexander's father replies, "We're prepared. John, do you need anything?"

"No, Urie. Thank you. I'm fine."

Urie gathers everyone up. "Let's get home. Your mother baked a German chocolate cake." Alexander and Leslie exchange looks. He has a big grin on his face as he moves both eyebrows up and down. "That sounds good." Leslie shoots a smile back at him.

They climb into the Hummer as John opens the garage door. Karl backs out. He waits until John has the door securely closed before he puts on the headlights and exits the property.

"Dad, should we reach out to Youngblood so he knows what's going on?"

"Not yet. Let me sleep on it. He'll need to be told about the key you fabricated, and that might drag John into this. He's a smart cop. Quite honestly, I'm surprised we haven't heard from him already."

Karl pulls up to the main house to let everyone in then returns to the carriage house, parking the Hummer in the underground garage.

Everyone is on their own for dinner tonight, scrounging up whatever they can find in the kitchen. About an hour later, they end up all together seated in the kitchen with coffee and cake including Carl and Karl.

Urie takes the floor. "We need to talk about what happened today. First, this was a professional hit. Second, they will come here. And third, we have to decide if we're going to sit and wait or take the fight to them."

Alexander is the first to answer. "We can't take the fight to them because we don't know who this hit man is or where his is. I vote for staying here to keep whatever's going to happen on our turf where we can stick together. After all, there is strength in numbers."

"What do you think, Karl and Carl?"

Karl offered his opinion, "I think it's a good idea to have them bring the fight to us. I'll be at the carriage house monitoring the property, and Carl will roam the property."

"Good, then it's decided. No closed doors tonight. We need to let the dogs roam. They can hear and smell things before we can."

Alexander speaks up, "We should probably get Bertoli in here tonight for downstairs."

"Already called him, son. He's on his way as we speak. Leslie, is it necessary for you to work tomorrow?"

"I wish I could say no, but I have a ton of things in process that need my attention tomorrow."

"Okay. Al, you go to work with Leslie tomorrow. Take Princess and run the boathouse job from there. Oh, as far as getting your truck from the apartment, I'll take care of that."

"Okay, dad, thanks."

Urie stands, "Well, everything seems to be settled." With that, the chatter turns to everyday topics.

21

Everyone eventually turns in, and as instructed, all the doors are left open. Leslie props pillows against the headboard as she sits in bed. The day's events play over and over again in her head. Princess is nowhere in sight, and she feels alone.

Two chimes sounded from the grandfather clock downstairs. She thinks a cup of hot chocolate might help her feel sleepy. She gets up and gazes out the french doors to decide if she is going to return to the kitchen or not. The harvest moon reveals the night's beauty shining so brightly; it creates shadows much like a sunny day. It looks to her like someone left a night-light on outside.

She makes up her mind. She's going down for that hot chocolate. That is, once she can tear herself away from looking outside. It is hypnotizing, like watching a fire in a fireplace. She's drawn into it, getting lost. Leslie's trance is broken by movement on the balcony. At first she questions whether or not her imagination is playing tricks on her. She stands very still, barely breathing when the moonlight reveals an intruder moving right for the french doors.

Involuntarily she backs up to the bed and makes herself as small as she possibly can. The canopy on her bed casts a shadow, and she sits in the darkness, invisible except for a small part of her foot which she slowly pulls into the shadows. She contemplates moving out of the room but changes her mind since it's too lit by the moon. She would definitely be seen. The intruder is now at the french door, which is locked.

Leslie's attention is drawn to the open door one more time as King silently glides through followed by Queen and Duke. Their movements are catlike, swift, as if called to this spot. Her fear builds when a wet nose nudges her hand. It's Princess. The dogs are still, stationary, statuelike. Leslie strains her eyes to pick them out against the dark background areas of the room.

Now there's a new sound, the slightest of clicks at one of the french doors right before it's opened. Leslie feels Princess tense as the intruder enters the room quietly without a sound. Only the moonlight gives him away. He's in the center of the room. King is first to grab him by the right wrist. Whatever he is holding hits the floor, and the momentum of the dog grabbing his wrist sends it in Leslie's direction. King's weight and strength easily turns the man around. The intruder lifts his left arm to hit King, but his swing never hit its mark. Queen intercepts. He is spinning in a circle struggling to stay upright as Duke grabs his leg, and that was it. His best effort cannot stop him from going down. Princess moves in. There is no barking or growling, in fact, there is very little noise. Leslie worries no one will know this intruder is here.

Just then the bedroom light goes on, and Urie comes in, pointing a gun at the intruder. Alexander is right behind his dad. Leslie climbs out of bed to look at the intruder, face down on the floor. King is holding his right wrist, Queen is holding his left wrist, Duke at one leg, and Princess positioned at the other.

Another man walks into the room with a walkie-talkie. Leslie never met him before, and she thinks he might be Bertoli.

"Bert, use the infrared camera on the path up to the lake."

"Yes, sir."

Urie has a walkie-talkie in his other hand, "Karl."

"Yes, boss."

"Turn the outside lights on."

Leslie looks outside as the night is turned into day. The silence is broken by the walkie-talkie.

"Urie."

"Yes, Bertoli."

"I'm picking up someone heading toward the lake."

"Karl, have your brother take the RTV to the lake. Be aware someone is on the path."

Urie looks down at the intruder. "Now, let's see what we have here. Can you hear me?"

"Yes."

"Good. I'm going to release the dogs. As soon as I do, you need to put your hands behind your back and don't make any other movements. Do you understand?"

"Yes."

"Good, release."

The dogs let go, but their eyes stay focused on each part of the body they held before his command.

"Okay, Al, handcuff him."

Alexander approaches the intruder, kneeling on his back and neck. He grabs one wrist at a time, bringing them to the center of his back as he places the cuffs tightly on him. He rocks back up to his feet and stands pulling the intruder up.

The silence is again broken by another walkie-talkie transmission. "Urie."

"Yes, Carl."

"I got up to the lake and caught a glimpse of him going down that old logging road. I followed, but he got into a vehicle heading toward town."

"Okay, Carl, good work. Come back to the main house to pick up our guest."

Olga pokes her head in the room. "Leslie, why don't we go downstairs and make some hot chocolate?"

"Sounds good. Be right with you."

"Alexander, take our guest down to Carl, please. Leslie, are you all right?"

"Yes, I am. You know, I've never been asked that question more often than since I met your son." She smiles affectionately at this family who took her under their wing.

"Let's head down to the kitchen. I think there's some leftover cake."

Urie picks up the intruder's gun then Leslie and Urie head arm in arm to the kitchen; the dogs follow.

Outside, Alexander hands the intruder over to Carl as Urie opens the door, letting the dogs outside.

"Hey, Carl, once you have our guest detained properly, take King and Duke to patrol around the house. Let your brother know I'll be over shortly."

"Yes, sir."

Leslie grabs Alexander as he enters the house. "I have questions, Al."

"Yes."

"How did you guys know that intruder was in my room?"

"Every door and window has a motion detector that registers movement in such a way that a leaf or a bird can't set it off. When the detector goes off, it alerts Karl and shows which location. Each detector has a small camera, so Karl can look at his monitor to see exactly what set if off. If he deems it's something of concern, he alerts my dad."

"But the dogs heard him?"

"In a way. All of the motion detectors have an alarm. Its sound is high like the pitch of a dog whistle, which you and I cannot hear. Each room has its own specific sound, which the dogs are trained to recognize, and that leads them to the room. Once inside, it's up to the dogs to identify which window or door is compromised."

"I've never heard of this type of system. Where did you buy it?"

"My dad designed, built, and installed it. So it's hard to get through it since there's no other system like it out on the market."

"I saw that man clearly out on the balcony. I felt sure he could see me too, but he didn't see me. I was afraid to run or make a move for the open door, thinking that would surely give me away."

"All the doors and windows are tinted. You could walk over to the bedroom door, and he would never see you."

"So if he couldn't see me, he wouldn't have been able to shoot me?"

"All the glass in the main and carriage house is bullet proof, but even if it wasn't, no one would chance the noise of breaking glass from a gunshot. He was here to kill us up front and personal with one shot, as close as possible."

Leslie questioned, "Who are these people?"

Before Alexander could speculate, Urie stuck his head in. "We're having coffee or hot chocolate, so come join us."

He took Leslie by the hand, and they vanished into the kitchen.

22

Urie and Alexander head over to the carriage house, leaving Queen and Princess behind with Olga and Leslie. Carl patrols the property with King and Duke. They enter the carriage house through a garage door located around back that leads to the basement. The intruder is secured to a metal chair fastened to the floor.

The setup has the feel of a gangland interrogation with an overhead flood. The light shines down on the intruder, creating a six-foot circle of light. Karl rests up against the pool table.

Urie stands just outside the circle of light and speaks to the intruder. "What were your plans?"

There is no response from the man. He continues to look straight ahead in Karl's direction.

"We know you can talk, so I'll ask you again, what were your plans?"

Still no response. Urie steps inside the circle of light where he pokes the intruder in the side of his head.

"Your plans?"

The intruder continues to stare at Karl without making a sound.

"I guess our friend is not going to talk," Karl says.

"We know you can hear us and understand our question. We will make you talk to us."

Urie backs out of the circle of light and says two words to Karl, "Prep him."

Karl pushes himself away from his resting place at the pool table, pulling out a knife. The intruder's eyes widen as sweat beads form on his upper lip and forehead. Karl begins his work by cutting off the intruder's shirt.

Alexander whispers to his father, "Why?"

"Karl likes to see the exact location to hit for maximum pain. I don't need this, but Karl does. That's why removing the shirt is important to his work."

Karl removes the last of the intruder's shirt, revealing a tattoo on his forearm which Alexander recognizes. "That tattoo. Wait a minute, I've seen it before. He's one of Figuora's men."

"How do you know that?"

"This tattoo of the cross with the serpent wrapped around it with the number on the cross is the same tattoo Skunk had. This man's number is sixty-two. I'm convinced that is how they confirm their identity to each other."

Urie and Karl look at Alexander, processing what he's just said, unsure what to think.

"Skunk is the guy we think killed Amy. He has that tattoo on his forearm too, but his number was eighty-two. I bet these people never know who they're sent to meet, so a tattoo is how they ID each other. The tattoo is the same, but the numbers are different."

Urie looks over the tattoo, speaking to the intruder, "So Figuora sent you?"

At that moment, Alexander put it all together. "No, dad, Figuora didn't send him. He was sent by Tomas Garcia."

For the first time since he is taken into the basement, the intruder moves his head to look at Alexander then struggles against his restraints, trying to get free.

Urie watches the intruder. "We know more about your drug-running system than you think."

The intruder's face goes wild, filled with anger, "You can't keep me. You must turn me over to the police," he yells.

His outburst draws laughter from Karl, who's removing his shirt. He is very muscular and, seeing him without his shirt, makes him appear even more formidable. Still chuckling, Karl walks toward the intruder. Urie knows everything Karl does is calculated and designed to intimidate. Karl is a master at evoking fear, and he does it well.

Karl shrugs. "No one knows you're here except your boss and us. I doubt you'll be missed." Karl is almost next to the intruder as he slides on a pair of brass knuckles.

"Yes," the intruder yells, "yes, there is someone else who knows I'm here. Detective Upton. I met him and he knows."

Urie steps back into the circle of light. "Actually, the good detective is next on our list, so why don't you save yourself some pain and give us some information."

"What will information buy me?"

"It depends on you. If no one gets hurt and we get Figuora, we'll turn you over to the police. If anyone in my family dies, you won't like the outcome."

Alexander watches his dad. He is so calm, but his words leave no doubt in anyone's mind that you need to take them seriously.

"Yes, Figuora is my boss, and I was sent here to reclaim the money that was taken and to teach your son and his girlfriend a valuable lesson."

Karl shifts his weight. "This we already know."

"Yes, Karl you're right. The next bit of information had better be something worthwhile that we don't know."

"I was not sent here alone. There was another man, the hit man."

"Just one?"

"Yes."

"That is the one that got away."

"So you know already."

"I do. So you see, you continue to tell me things we already know."

Urie turns away from the intruder and, walking toward Alexander, says, "Let's go, Alexander."

It's clear the intruder doesn't like his odds if he's left alone with

Karl, so before Urie and Alexander leave, he calls out, "Wait, there is a large shipment coming up next week. Larger than any other moved through here so far."

This stops Urie in his tracks. "Why now?"

"Burlington is no longer going to be safe with everything that's happened. So the Garcia's are pushing it along to a new location following that shipment. They're tying up loose ends, and you and your wife have been targeted."

"Where is this second man who was here with you now?"

"At the rectory, but not for long."

"Karl, put our guest back in his room but, before you do, teach him a lesson. Don't break anything or kill him since we still need him for now."

The intruder struggles again against his restraints, "But I gave you something. Something you didn't know!"

"Yes, that's true. That is why you will not die tonight, but you came after my son and our future daughter-in-law. I can't let this happen. You need to understand that. Come, Al."

Urie and Alexander exit the basement. "I'm concerned about this second man. Take the ATV and Carl up to the cabin. Let's be sure this second man is gone. Be careful, son. These people are very dangerous."

Alexander and Carl drop him off at the main house. Urie stands watching them head up the mountain until they're out of sight. He looks up into the sky to see it's starting to get light. There will be no sleep tonight. Urie turns and walks into the kitchen. The girls are busy baking, filling the air with the smells of their labor and freshly brewed coffee.

Urie helps himself to a cup of coffee, and pulling Youngblood's business card out of his pocket, he dials his number.

Dressed and ready to leave for the precinct, Youngblood's cell phone rings. "Youngblood."

"It's Urie Acof, Sergeant Youngblood. You said to call you if we need anything."

"Good morning, Urie. It's early; what's up?"

"We had some trouble at our home last night. I need you here."

"I'll be there in thirty minutes."

23

Youngblood skids on the dirt road leading to the Acof property, almost launching him past the entrance. The dirt road forces him to slow down, but he continues at a good clip. Karl sees his rooster tail from the carriage house and walks outside to meet Youngblood as he arrives. Youngblood slows once he sees Karl, who waves him over to the main house.

Pulling up to the main house, Youngblood spots Alexander by the front door. Climbing out of his vehicle, he says, "I hear you had trouble last night."

"We did, sergeant. Please come in. My father will fill you in on everything." Alexander escorts Youngblood into the kitchen where they join Urie, Olga, and Leslie who are already seated at the table.

Youngblood smiles and offers a good morning to everyone and takes a seat. Olga places some coffee and freshly baked pound cake in front of him.

"So shall we get down to why you called me here? What happened, Urie?"

"I need to tell you some things and ask some questions too.

Youngblood, you're good at what you do, one of our better policemen, and some of the things I plan to share may not be what you want to hear. No matter what you decide, there are things me and my family have to do. But first, that explosion at Leslie's apartment, do you know what caused it?"

"I was told it was a gas leak in the kitchen stove."

"Did you see the damage in the apartment for yourself? Are you sure a gas leak caused it?"

"The fire department investigator isn't sure, but it's clear he felt the pressure to put something down. I do know the damage was quite extensive." Looking at Leslie and Alexander, he added, "You were very lucky to get out of there."

"That's curious, don't you think? I mean, after all, a lot of natural gas would have to leak out to cause extensive damage. You'd think someone in the complex would have smelled it, yet according to my sources, no one came forward."

"Yes, you would think so, Urie. I have to ask you, what is your theory?"

Alexander hands the backpack to Youngblood and Urie nods, nonverbally telling him to look inside. He did as asked and pulled out three thermal grenades, a .22 automatic with a silencer and extra clips. Youngblood places each item on the table. "How did you come by this?"

"Two men were sent here last night to take care of us, but we foiled their plans. One of the intruders got away."

"The obvious questions, what happened to the other man if one got away and any idea who sent them?"

"Figuora did," Alexander replies.

Youngblood turns to face Alexander. "How can you be so certain?"

"Our intruder told us. He's still here if you want to verify this information."

"Where is he, Urie? Can I see him?"

"You can, sergeant, all in due time. He also has the tattoo of the serpent with the cross on his forearm. His displays the number sixty-two on it."

Youngblood is quiet for a moment, thinking this theory they've been building has been right all along. But there is one thing that keeps nagging at him because it doesn't make sense. "Why would Figuora get so bold that he would do this?"

Everyone is quiet as his observation hangs in the air until Urie gets up to enter the walk-in freezer. He returns with a green duffle bag which he places in front of Youngblood. Watching Youngblood open the duffle, he breaks the silence, "There is $380,000 dollars in there. We believe it was on its way back to Mexico when my son intercepted it. Plus our intruder tells us the Garcias no longer feel Burlington is safe, so their doing one last very large drug shipment. It's the biggest one to date, and it's coming through next week. After that, they'll be gone."

Youngblood is speechless. Urie adds, "Even more importantly, my family is scheduled for another visit."

"I don't want to know how you got this money, but I do want to know if you believe the other information is credible?"

"Unfortunately, yes. Youngblood, I know you shared with my son that you haven't told anyone about any of this. Is that still true? Have you since told your captain?"

"No, but after I leave here, I will need to tell him something. I'm just unsure exactly what or how much. I waited because I wanted to keep all of you safe."

"No need to worry about that any longer. There is a select few of us who know what's going on. You'd be better served to worry about the existence of a second hit man somewhere in town."

"I can have a police detail set up here if you like."

Urie is slow to answer for a moment. He nods his agreement with this offer. "Maybe stationing a patrol car down at the entrance would suffice. Thank you. I hope you take precautions too, sergeant, because you're as much a target as we are."

"Yes, I know. If it's okay with you, I'd like to see this intruder now."

"Follow me." Urie leads him to the door pausing at the intercom. "Karl, I'm bringing Sergeant Youngblood over to see the intruder."

As they walk over to the carriage house, Youngblood suggests he release the intruder into his custody.

"Sergeant, I cannot release him to you. I took a chance letting you know he's here out of respect. This man knows more than he's shared, and I want to get more out of him. I'd ask you to be more concerned over the safety of my family. Can you guarantee their safety?"

Youngblood didn't say a word as they walked through the garage door behind the carriage house into the basement. Before they went further, Youngblood stopped Urie, "Is he alive?"

"Yes, of course."

"Will I like what I'm going to see?"

"Probably not, but no one is coming here with the intention of hurting my family without some retribution."

Youngblood stood there evaluating what Urie said. On one level, he understood what he's feeling, but he's also conflicted by his vows as a policeman.

Karl opens the basement door, and they walk in. Youngblood is flooded with questions. "Is there a possibility this intruder can escape?"

"No, we have him in a cinderblock cold cellar; no windows. He is sitting on a mattress, and his legs are chained to an eyebolt anchored in the cement floor. The only exit is through the heavy metal door that's barred close and monitored."

Youngblood places his hand on Urie's arm, stopping their forward progress. "If I go in there and don't like what I see, I'll be inclined to bring him back with me to the precinct; and once I tell the captain about what's going on, he'll expect me to bring him in."

Youngblood shifts his gaze between Urie and Karl standing by the metal door. He continues, "A guy like that doesn't give up information just because you ask him. It's better to use a certain technique, shall we say, and Karl has that?"

Urie responds as Karl does not generally partake in any conversation without prompting. "Sergeant, all the information he gave us so far came freely without our needing to really rough him up."

"You're telling me you never laid a hand on him for the information?"

"That's correct, I did not. He felt a need to bargain with us when we encouraged him to do so." Urie assures him.

Youngblood read between the lines and made his decision. "I'm not going in to see him because if I do and I see something I don't like, I'll be forced to take him out of here."

"I need him here. He knows more. I suggest you tell your captain he got away. Take the money, grenades, and the gun; that should be enough to convince him."

Youngblood points his finger from one man to the other. "You don't touch him. No torture. He stays alive, got it?"

Urie nods to Karl, and for the first time, he speaks, "Mr. Acof says do nothing then it's nothing."

Youngblood turns to leave. "I have to get downtown. I'll be in touch." Urie and Karl walk him out. "If you get any more information, call me."

"No problem. I gave you everything I have so far. It does me no good to hold back when my family is at risk."

Youngblood shakes his head in agreement. With that, he starts his car and drives off. Once he's out of sight, Karl turns to Urie, "What do I do with our guest?"

"Clean him and patch him up, put a new shirt on him to cover the bruising. Take good care of him for right now."

24

On his ride to the precinct, Youngblood replays all the facts. He wants to prepare by anticipating as many questions as possible along with exactly how much information he should share. Upon his arrival, Youngblood gets out of his cruiser and stands, looking at the building. Leaning against the doorframe with his arm on the roof, he wonders how everything got so out of control. Lost in concentration, he's brought back into the moment by someone calling out his name. It is Charles Upton heading straight for him.

"I need to talk with you." Upton calls out as he closes the distance between them. "Can't it wait. Charles? I need to speak with the captain."

Upton is now inside his personal space. "How urgent can it be, Youngblood? A minute ago you were standing here staring into space. But what can be so important? It's about Figuora, isn't it?"

The hair on the back of Youngblood's neck is standing on end. Was Charles sent to stop him? The words spoken earlier resonate in his mind, reminding him he is a target too.

"Why exactly are you here, Charles?"

"I'm in too deep and I need to talk. Please. I know I'm not one of your favorite people, but I'm asking you, just hear me out."

"Okay, Charles, let's go inside and talk." He is very aware that Upton is nervous and jumpy. "Not here. I'll buy you a cup of coffee."

Youngblood still has his car door open. "Get in." They drive over to the Champlain Diner and sit in a back booth and order coffee, silently waiting for it to be delivered. Once it's set down and the waitress walks away, Youngblood asks Upton, "What's so important, Charles?"

"Figuora's not who he pretends to be."

"I know, Charles. His real name is Tomas Garcia, a drug runner, and he had those football players try to teach Alexander a lesson that failed. He sent hit men to take out the Acofs, which I might add failed, but they got away. What else can you add?"

Upton is uncomfortable, taken aback by how much Youngblood has figured out. "Not a whole hell of a lot."

"The football players, why would they do Figuora's bidding?"

"He supplies them with steroids. They want to go to big colleges on scholarship with plans to go pro. Are you sure both hit men got away?"

"Yup, what else have you got? Why did you bring me here?"

"I became friends with that homeless guy named Skunk. He needed money once or twice when he got into minor trouble, and I helped him out. I got information by throwing him a couple of bucks here and there. It wasn't until after we were friendly that he told me he worked for Figuora. Told me he had him on a short leash. Skunk lived in the rectory basement."

"Why would he want to give you information, Charles, especially with the setup he had?"

"He wanted out of this town, out from under Figuora. He wanted to bring his girl up from Mexico so the two of them could disappear."

Youngblood sat there looking at Charles. He figured Charles is trapped, but he also knew he is being played.

"How could you be so stupid, Charles? Did you kill Skunk and that other guy?"

"No, Figuora did that to keep his hands in it, so he won't lose his touch or his reputation for being tough. He's going to tie me into one or both of the murders somehow. I'm sure of it."

"I can see Skunk's murder, but how would he get you on to the other guy?"

"I gave him to Figuora. That guy was using drugs, and he would agree to anything for the right deal. I never thought he'd kill him. I knew his organization was pushing the drugs through Burlington, and at first, I wanted this bust. I was so close and then that damn Alexander and Leslie threw a monkey wrench into everything."

"We need to go to the captain, Charles." Youngblood doesn't know whether or not to believe this version of what happened. He is doubtful that Charles it telling the absolute truth, but without evidence, there is nothing he can do. Pushing him to meet with the captain is a good place to start.

"I can't."

"Charles, the captain is going to learn what's going on sooner or later, and sooner from us is better. I promised Mr. Acof protection for his family, and I have to go through the captain to get it."

Youngblood knows he needs to convince Charles, plus this would get him off the street for a while and eliminate Figuora trying to blackmail him into another one of his dirty deeds as all the details unfold.

"You're not hearing me. I can't."

"Charles, better if he hears about this from us. Don't you want him to know about your intentions? Don't be a dumbass."

Across town, Figuora calls Mexico to fill Carlos in on what's going on in Burlington. "Hola, Tomas. Glad to hear from you. How are you?"

"Everything is in place for the shipment next week, Carlos. After it's done, I want out of here quick."

"Slow down, my brother. We'll get you out. Just make certain all the product gets shipped and all the money gets here to me. Do you understand?"

Tomas did not tell his brother about the failed hit on the Acofs and the girl. When it comes to money, Carlos is not at all understanding. He keeps his tone even so Carlos cannot pick up on anything.

"Everything is on schedule."

"This better happen, Tomas, or I will be very unhappy and that includes the money we're missing."

They agreed the two hit men will remain in Burlington until the job of getting the money back is complete and said their good-byes. Tomas knew things were going bad, but he couldn't stop the biggest shipment from coming, plus all the mules were already in motion. He is hoping to deal with the Acofs in a way that will give him the extra time he needs right now to press Upton into getting the missing money. He decides now is a good time to play that card.

Back at the diner, Upton's cell phone rings. He looks at the display but makes no move to answer the call.

"Who is it, Charles?"

"It's Figuora."

"You need to answer it, Charles. Remember, he has people in town. People who can easily take you out. You have to answer it and keep everything casual."

Charles answers his call. It is Figuora pressuring him to get the missing money. Youngblood listens as he tells Figuora it is he who screwed up not him. He also asks him how he's expected to fix what his professional hit men couldn't do. He let him know the money may very well be in police custody for all he knew.

Youngblood watches as Upton's demeanor changes, and Charles is promising to make the money disappear from the evidence lockup if it is actually there and then disconnected the call.

Youngblood can tell by Upton's body language things did not go well. "Let me guess, Figuora wants you to get the money."

"Yes. Let me have it to buy time."

"No, Charles. I'm going to see the captain, and I strongly suggest you go with me."

25

Neither speaks as they head up the precinct stairs. Upton is sweating profusely. As they exit the stairwell into the upper level, the captain is there standing before them.

"I've been looking for the two of you. In my office, now."

The captain holds open his office door for them, following he sits at his desk. "What the hell, may I ask, is going on?"

Youngblood takes the lead. "Father Figuora from Saint Gerard's is running drugs through Burlington out to larger cities." And with that intro, he did his best to update the captain on everything he knew and everything he suspected, at least within reason for this moment in time.

He shares how Upton is trying to infiltrate this drug cartel on his own but manages to get in deeper and deeper, how Leslie and Alexander accidentally discover this drug network following Amy's death, and finally, how they did not bring this to him earlier because they were looking to get more evidence while protecting Leslie and Alexander.

The captain leans back in his chair, thinking about what he's just learned. Without saying a word, he stands, goes to his office door, and calls out, "Sergeant Gilbert!" Returning, he sits at his desk, leaving the door ajar.

"Charles, I want your gun and shield." He folds his hands on his desk blotter waiting for Charles to make his move. Upton places both items on his desk without saying a word. A knock on the door causes them to stop staring at each other for the first time during this exchange.

It's Sergeant Gilbert. "You called for me, cap?"

"Put Charles here in one of our holding cells." Looking at Charles, the captain said, "Charles, I am doing this for a few reasons, but the most important reasons are to keep you out of trouble for a while and somewhere where I can easily find you."

"Gilbert, make certain he has nothing he can use to hurt himself." And with that, they were gone.

Now the captain turns his attention to Youngblood. "I'm not too pleased with you either, Youngblood. I'm rethinking my decision to not put you in a holding cell right next to him."

Youngblood understands and knew from the start this meeting with the captain was destined to be challenging. "I need a patrol car assigned to the end of the Acof driveway. The hit men tried once, and we don't have a line on them, but I'm closing in. Captain, I know you're not happy with me, but I need to work this case."

"This whole case is just wrong, Youngblood. Do you know how concerned the Turners are? I'm not happy, and you can only imagine how they're feeling."

Youngblood nodded his head. "Just give me the freedom to work this case."

The captain points his finger at Youngblood. "I'm in the loop from here on or you're in the other holding cell."

"Yes, sir."

"Now do me a favor and get the hell out of here before I change my mind."

26

Figuora paces back and forth in his office. He needs a trump card, something to get everyone's attention to insure he gets what he needs. Father Payne sits on the couch in front of the window. Figuora's not worried about Father Clarkson. There's no way he will give up any information. Both of these men are professionals, trained to endure pain. No one without specific skills will get anywhere with him.

"Figuora, let me go back to the Acof mansion. I will get in. I'll put fear into these people. Clarkson tripped up somehow. It has to be a glitch. I don't know. Maybe he stepped on a twig or the stairs squeaked, but no matter, I'm better at breaking and entering."

"No, Payne. It's not that simple. There has to be something there, something none of us anticipated."

"I know there's motion detectors on the doors and windows. They won't pick you up if you move slow enough. I mean, all detectors allow for movement to a certain degree. Clarkson would have set off the alarm right away, but he was inside the mansion. The dogs never heard him. I'm telling you, he was inside. He had to make a mistake. We were all over the property the night before. We went right up to some of the windows and a door. If the dogs didn't get wind of us, they wouldn't have known we were there."

"No alarm?"

"Nope. The dogs began to bark, but we never set off the motion detectors."

"I'm uncomfortable with this family. They stopped my powerful football players, and the odds were in my favor of three to one. The Acof's son, Alexander, took them out, and this shouldn't have happened. The other thing that bothers me is those two gardeners. One of them is always with the old man while the other always patrols the property."

"You're making them sound superhuman. Maybe they are for some things, but a bullet to the back of the head stops a rhino."

Figuora doesn't answer, unable to shake feeling uncomfortable. He needs something special, a new plan. Maybe Leslie or Alexander's mom can make this work, but getting to either of them is a challenge. That house must have something they're missing, and during the day at the studio, they have a dog with them. That leaves Alexander who travels alone; and now Upton is missing, not answering his cell phone, making him wonder how much the police know. He will make his plan assuming they know everything, no matter how they got there.

Payne breaks the silence. "Let me go in, Frank."

"Listen, Payne, I think they know about us and what's going on here in Burlington. I'm not sure how, but I think they know."

"How is that possible, Frank? I think you're being paranoid. And even if you are right, we need to move on to the next plan of action. What can we do to get their attention? It's got to be really good."

"In the next two to three days, I have over thirty mules coming in with the product. It's the biggest shipment we ever pushed through this area. We need to repack it and ship it out with the money collected."

"I know. What's your point? Will you be sending the money back using the usual way?"

"Not this time. We need to hold on to it, and you and I will bring it back to Carlos. We have to move our operation out of the rectory and over to the warehouse right now. I have most of the homeless over there already. I've been moving out of here little by little ever since the Peter's girl was murdered. This way, neither the boys nor Mrs. O'Brien were the wiser. We need to finish up the move today."

"What's going on with Brad, Leon, and Rock?"

"They're no good for this work anymore. That last fiasco clinched that for us. So the question is what will stop the people who know too much about our operation? Really stop them and give us the time we need to get this last shipment in and out before we take another hit?"

"I'm not sure, Figuora."

An evil grin materializes on Figuora's face. All roads bring him back to this. "The only way to put a hold on things is to get either Leslie or Mrs. Acof, maybe even both of them. That will give us the upper hand again. Maybe getting to Leslie is not so hard after all since I have just the right tool here in the rectory, Mrs. O'Brien."

Both men sit smiling now.

"Payne, get Mrs. O'Brien in here now." It may not be the best plan, but it feels just like what he needs. He turns as Mrs. O'Brien walks into his office.

"Father Figuora, Father Payne tells me you need me?"

"Yes, I need to talk with you. Father Payne, can you close the office door on your way out, please?"

Mrs. O'Brien watches the door close, and they listen to the footsteps retreating.

"Father Figuora, I don't trust that priest. He leaves me feeling uneasy."

"I don't trust him either, but when the diocese sends someone, you have no real input. Oh well. The reason why I need to speak with you is about one of our own. Leslie Turner. Her parents called me and asked me to talk with her since she refuses to talk to them about what happened to her friend Amy. They are very concerned about her."

"She is a wonderful girl, and she really should talk."

"Yes, I agree. I actually went over to the studio the other day, but she broke down sobbing. We didn't make any headway, so I hugged her; and when I did, I smelled alcohol on her breath. That's what has me so concerned. She really needs to talk before this thing gets out of hand."

Mrs. O'Brien is wringing her hands. "That's not like her, Father."

"Yes, I know. She needs to understand that bad things happen in life, and if it's true that Skunk was involved in Amy's death as I've heard, then it's my fault for having him here. Maybe Amy would still be alive if things we're different."

"Father, don't second guess yourself. You were just trying to do some good. Is there anything I can do to help?"

"I am hoping you can. Will you call her and invite her over to talk? Or better still, tell her that you need to talk and you're alone at the rectory. If she asks, tell her I am out and not returning until tomorrow. I fear she won't come if she knows I'm here."

"I will, Father."

Figuora picks up the phone receiver, hands it to Mrs. O'Brien, and dials the studio. Leslie answers the call on the third ring.

"Hello, Leslie, it's Mrs. O'Brien."

"Hi, Mrs. O'Brien. How are you?"

"I'm not doing real well. I need to talk with someone, and I'm hoping it can be you. How about I put on some tea? I'm alone here, and what I need to talk about concerns you. Father Figuora won't be back until tomorrow, so I have to be here and can't come to you."

Leslie could not disappoint her. She is like a mother to her, better than her own. "I'll be right there. Give me about twenty minutes."

"Good. Thank you, Leslie, I'll be in the kitchen waiting for you."

Mrs. O'Brien hands the receiver back to Father Figuora. "She is on her way. I feel so dishonest, Father."

"No, this is really fantastic. She needs this. I'm calling her parents to have them come over too. Tell you what, maybe you should sit in when we talk."

"I would like that, Father. Leslie is like a daughter to me. I better get back to the kitchen. I have an apple pie in the oven, and it will come in handy."

"Good, that's good. This will work out. Can you send Father Payne back in for me?" Mrs. O'Brien walks out, and passing Father Payne in the hall, sends him back to the office.

"Yea."

"Good news, Leslie is on her way here. Take the van up the street and get back here as quickly as you can."

27

Leslie pulls up to the rectory, sitting in her car, wondering if she should actually be here. She thinks about how she promised Youngblood she'd stay away. The difference is she's not here to snoop. She's here for a friend, a friend in need.

Leslie gets out of her car walking toward the side entrance of the rectory. The door is unlocked, and she heads for the kitchen. Mrs. O'Brien is bent over the stove. She smiles at Leslie and closes the oven door gingerly.

"Leslie, thank you for coming."

"Is everything okay?"

"It is now that you're here, dear. Let's have some tea."

"I can't stay too long, but I have time for tea."

Mrs. O'Brien's smile fades, making Leslie turn to see what she is looking at. It's Father Figuora. He is standing in the doorway. Leslie heads for the stairs. Opening the kitchen door, she comes face-to-face with Father Payne who puts his arms around her, carrying her back into the kitchen.

Mrs. O'Brien cannot understand what is going on, and she says loudly, "There's no need for that."

Father Figuora drops his angelic persona. "Shut up, Mrs. O'Brien." And he gets to work with his duct tape. He binds Leslie's hands and feet, pushing her to the floor, and follows the same steps with Mrs. O'Brien. Both women have a terrified look in their eyes.

"Payne, get the van."

Payne leaves the rectory, going up the street to retrieve the van. He backs it up to the side entrance, opens the rear doors, and reenters the kitchen.

"Throw them in the van, Payne."

"Do we really need the old one?"

"She may come in handy so take them both. Make sure to tie them down, so they can't escape."

Payne did as instructed, securing Leslie first followed by Mrs. O'Brien. He locks the van's rear doors and climbs into the driver's seat. He patiently waits for Figuora, who climbs in a few minutes later, carrying a small bag.

"Head for the warehouse."

Leslie and Mrs. O'Brien can only look at each other. Neither of them can do nor see anything. They can feel the van start and turn left, which meant they head north. It takes about fifteen minutes to get to where they're going without too many turns. Leslie thinks she may have an idea where they're going. She commits as many details as she can to her memory; the van turns left then right, crosses railroad tracks, straight, left again then slows to a stop. The horn is blown, and she hears a garage door open. The van moves forward, and the engine is turned off. She hears both front doors open, and both men exit. The garage door is closed.

Payne follows Figuora to the office in front of the warehouse.

"What do we do now? Should we call to let them know we have Leslie?"

Figuora shakes his head. "Not yet. Let's let them wonder where she is for a while."

"Okay, but what if she told someone she was going to the rectory?"

"At this point, it doesn't really matter. I have her, and that's all that matters. Send someone to the rectory to get her car. Check on the others and make sure they are finished removing their things from the rectory. Remind everyone to stay clear of that location. No one can go back there no matter what. Put the old bird in the back room tied to a chair. Bring Leslie here to me."

Payne gets to work. He takes care of the old one first. Once finished, he gets Leslie up and cuts the duct tape from her ankles so she can walk on her own. Exiting the van, Leslie counts eight people who look homeless. Payne shoves her in the direction of the front office. He opens the door and pushes her in.

"Leslie, please take a seat," Father Figuora tells her.

Figuora slides a chair over in her direction. She hears Figuora instruct Payne to make sure everyone is fed. She sees the only exit from the office is the door they came through. She turns her head to look out the side window. The building next door is all brick, quite ornate, giving Leslie the feeling she's been here before. She replays the way they drove here in her mind and thinks this location is close to John's pawnshop. She can feel it. It has to be.

Figuora turns back into the office and shuts the door behind him. He looks at Leslie and, walking over, pulls the duct tape off of her mouth.

"Okay, Leslie. You will be fine as long as you are a good girl."

"If Alexander were here, he…"

Figuora cuts her off in midsentence. "He's not here, and he has no idea you are even missing, let alone where you are. Before you start, you need to know Mrs. O'Brien's life depends on you and how you act. If you don't cooperate, we will hurt her."

Leslie is in a bad nightmare. If only she could wake up.

Payne returns. "We need you out there."

Figuora gets up to leave. "Leslie, I'll be right back. A word to the wise: be good."

Leslie tries to gain control of herself. Her thoughts racing, she thinks about Alexander and the three football players that attacked him. He wasn't scared. She needs to do the same, stay in control and think. The best plan will be for her to get herself and Mrs. O'Brien out of here. She believes they're near the pawnshop and help.

Looking out the glass in the office door, she spots boxes of canned goods, vegetables, fruit, Spam and other household items. This must be the bulk of the food from the food pantry. She can hear the garage door open and the sound of a vehicle entering. The garage door closes. There is talking outside the office, but she cannot make out what the muffled voices are saying. Footsteps approach, the office door is opened by Payne, who grabs her and leads her out of the office and down a narrow hallway to the left. She can tell he's taking her to the rear of the warehouse. The hallway is lined with boxes and tools on both side walls. There is another door on the left, and Payne pushes her in. She trips and falls. Payne is impatient and grabs her hair to pull her to her feet. He puts her into an old-style wooden desk chair with a high back, arm rests, wheels. It is the kind of chair one can imagine behind a roll top desk. It looks like the chair her favorite nun Space Ghost had in the fourth grade.

Her wrists are still duct taped. Payne pushes her legs together to duct tape them around the ankles. He adds two bungee cords to her waist around the chair and places another strip of duct tape across her mouth. Lifting his leg, he places his foot on the chair and shoves it across the room. Leslie lands in the corner of the room, hitting her head on a wooden stud.

Payne looks at her and laughs, leaving her there in the dark. Once Leslie's eyes adjust, she sees Mrs. O'Brien is in here with her. The room has two windows. One on each wall. They are both boarded up, but the space between the boards allows light to beam through. The dust they kicked up dances in the streams of light. The room has a brown color to it with a table by the door. There are bungee cords and duct tape on it.

The rear window is broken with a small shard of glass on the window sill. She can see more glass on the floor. Each board is held in place with what appears to be Phillips head screws. She almost wants to laugh at this observation since she would not recognize a Phillips head screw before Alexander. Just the thought of him calms her. She is doing what he would do, getting to know her surroundings. She notices the quiet.

Digging her heels into the floor, she pulls herself over to Mrs. O'Brien. She looks scared. She cannot move her hands enough to touch her arm. The air is cold and neither of them is dressed for it.

Figuora and Payne sit in the front office. They have their people moving in and out. Product is coming in and going out. All money received gets locked in the van by Figuora. So far, he estimates he has between seven and eight million. This does not include the money the police have in their evidence room.

Father Figuora tells Payne, "I think we will ask for a ransom on Leslie for $380,000 plus. This way, we'll get our money back and more. I'll have Alexander take it out to a drop site. Then while he is detained and tied up, you'll go to the Acof mansion."

"I'm ready for that."

"Then we'll bring all this money plus some back to Carlos. He will be very happy."

28

It is almost 7:00 p.m. and she's not back. Olga worries about Leslie, and she can't wait any longer; it's time to call Alexander.

"Yes, Mom, what's up?'

"Have you heard from Leslie?'

"No, why do you ask? Isn't she with you?"

"She got a call and left here several hours ago. She said there was something she had to do, and she'd be right back."

"Did she take Princess with her?"

"No, she ran out of here before I could find out where she was going. That was three hours ago."

"Call, Dad. I'm on my way."

Alexander wastes no time heading to the studio. He finds his mother standing outside. Alexander parks and walks her back inside. He can tell she is worried, and he tries not to show that he feels the same way. It is time to keep his wits about himself.

"This is not like her. I know she got a phone call, and I wasn't really paying attention; but right after she hung up, she left here."

"It's not your fault, Mom. Did you call Dad?"

"Yes. He wants us to come home. He said he is going to call Youngblood to tell him what is going on. Everyone knows it's not like Leslie to do something like this, especially following what happened to Amy."

Looking out the front window, they see Youngblood arrive. He is on his cell phone. Once inside the studio, he puts it away.

"I spoke with your husband, and he filled me in. I sent a patrol car over to the rectory in case that's where she went. The odd thing is no one is there, not even Mrs. O'Brien. That can't be right. The captain agrees with me, and he sent several men over to search the rectory. Did she mention anything about where she was going? Could it have been to see a customer?"

Olga shakes her head no. "She never said. All she said is she'd be back in one hour. That was about 4:00 p.m."

Alexander paces. "Leslie is not like that. She always calls when she's running late, plus she came in today with my mom in one car. It doesn't make sense."

Youngblood calls the precinct to place an APB on her vehicle. Alexander knows Figuora is involved somehow. He is wondering how he got to her. Why did she let her guard down?

"We're doing all we can right now. So for starters, I need the two of you to go home. I'm going to the rectory to join the search. Once I'm done there, I'll come over to your house. If she calls you, call me right away."

Youngblood heads for the front door of the studio. He stops, turns, looks at them, saying one word, "Home."

Alexander turns off the lights, sets the alarm, and locks the door. Both dogs stand by his truck, waiting for him to let them in. Both dogs jump in, but his mom is not moving. He knows she doesn't want to leave the studio. Eventually she gives in, and they head toward home. Youngblood leaves at the same time, but he goes off in the direction of the rectory.

As Alexander approaches the driveway, there is a patrol car parked to the side. He pulls around it, nodding at the policemen. He drives slowly up to the closed carriage house gates. They wait, and Carl appears to open them. Olga never utters one word. As Alexander slows the truck in front of the mansion, she opens the door and jumps out. The vehicle had not even come to a complete stop. Both dogs rush toward the house.

Alexander follows the voices inside the house to his father's study.

"Honey, you have to do something. Whoever did this must pay. We need Leslie home now."

"I'm prepared, dear, but we don't know where they are. If they took her, it's because they want something; otherwise, she would be dead."

Olga stands there, not liking what he had to say, but she knows he's right. His words are hard to accept. Alexander stands in the hall. Filled with anger, he is challenged to keep it under control. He knows his dad is right. Right now there is nothing they can do. He hopes Figuora wants something from them. He enters the study and sits in front of the fireplace.

"Honey, can you make us some coffee and perhaps bring some pound cake?"

"Who can eat at a time like this?" Olga heads for the kitchen. Maybe she should just bake. She'll feel better doing something normal, and the kitchen is her favorite room in their home.

"Do you believe Figuora wants something?"

"I do, Al. In the very least, he'll want his $380,000 back. He may even push that amount higher as a ransom for Leslie."

"The police won't give the money back to us. Can we get that amount of money together if we need to?"

"I have people working on that now. We can get up to 1.2 million in cash if we need it. I have another contact in Russia, but that will take time."

The telephone rings, and Alexander grabs for it. It is apparent he feels very edgy. Urie puts his hand on top of his, telling him to calm down. Urie answers the phone.

"Hello, Sergeant Youngblood. Yes, we're all here. Sure. Come right over. We're in the study." Urie hangs up the phone and grabs the walkie-talkie. He instructs Karl to tell Carl about Youngblood's arrival and to get ready to let him enter at the gate. He also tells him to move the prisoner from his room to the chair since more pressing conversation needs to take place.

Al, having listened to his father's conversations, asks if he can help in any way.

"I know this is tough. First, let's see what Youngblood has to say. We're on lockdown. Carl continuously roams with the dogs; his brother is at the monitors watching the house. After Youngblood leaves, we'll see what our prisoner knows. I bet they have a safe house somewhere in the Burlington area. It just makes sense with all these people coming in and going out."

"When I was staking out the rectory, the only direction they would continually go in is north. Do you think I should go out looking around in that area?"

"No, Alexander. If something comes up, I'll need you. There are too many locations north of the rectory. You'll end up spinning your wheels."

He feels disappointed, preferring to be doing something other than sitting and waiting. His mom returns and sits next to him on the couch. Both of them get lost in their thoughts watching the fire. It's clear that everyone is concerned about Leslie and her safe return.

Youngblood drives up toward the carriage house. As he approaches the gate, Carl is there to open them and directs him to the main house. Youngblood parks, climbs the stairs, and heads toward the study. He sits down with the Acofs by the fireplace.

"There is nothing at the rectory. No maps, schedules, or anything else down in the basement. The kitchen oven door was open with two apple pies inside; the oven was off. No drugs but our drug-sniffing dog went crazy, so we know there was stuff there recently. Every aspect indicates they left in a hurry."

Urie is done with him. He stands and says, "Thank you, sergeant. I need to talk with my family."

Youngblood understood. "If I get anything else, I'll be in touch." With that said, he leaves. Youngblood needs to talk to Upton. Maybe he knows something useful.

Once Youngblood is out of sight, Urie heads for the carriage house. Alexander follows right behind. They head for the basement, knowing Carl will have everything in place.

29

Youngblood heads back to the precinct. He's going to stay on good terms with the captain, starting with the interrogation of Upton.

"Cap, you got a minute?"

"Yea, come on in. How did the Acofs take what's happened?"

"They're not happy. Urie's putting money together just in case there's a ransom."

"I'm against that, Youngblood. What did you say to them when they told you? Did you recommend it?"

"Nope, but they need to feel like they're doing something. I'm thinking if I interrogate Upton, maybe I'll get information preventing the need for ransom."

"How's that?"

"If Father Figuora has Leslie, and let's say he's going to ask for a ransom, I mean he is out the $380,000, they had to take her somewhere in this area. They're not at the rectory; they must have another location, and maybe Upton knows something about where it is." His logic makes sense to the captain.

"But what if they left town?"

"I don't think he left town. First, he has no way of knowing how much we know, so he'll want to be close to his cover, plus Urie is right, he's going to ask for money. I think Upton may know something."

"Okay, let's do it! Gilbert!" the captain yells. Looking at Youngblood he says, "The only thing is you're not going to interrogate him because I am."

Gilbert comes running and stops in front of the captain, awaiting his orders. "Gilbert, put our boy Charles into interrogation room number one."

Youngblood makes one last ditch effort to be the man doing the interrogating. "Cap, it has to be me with Upton. He'll tell me more than he'll tell you. I should do it."

"Harold, as of right now, there will be an inquiry into the actions of both of you regarding this case. You're looking at some rough waters ahead, believe me. If I let you interrogate him, it's my ass in a sling. They'd accuse me of being out of line, and I'm not putting my ass in jeopardy for you or anyone else."

Harold wishes it could be different, but he understands. He offers to help with the preparation. He sits down with the captain to go over the facts, and they walk together toward interrogation room number one. Youngblood slips into the adjacent viewing room.

"You know, captain, you can't keep holding me here like this." Upton doesn't want to push the issue. He's sure they don't have much on him, but the uncertainty is there.

"Charles, we need to talk, and until I know your part in all this, I'm holding you. Plus it will keep you from getting into any further trouble. We think Figuora has Leslie Turner. You know who I'm talking about, right, Charles?"

"You know I do."

"Well, Figuora's left the comfort of the rectory, retreating to another location, hopefully in town. Charles, it'll go a long way if you step up to help us now. Do you know where this other location might be?"

Charles wants to tell him everything he knows, and he'd love Figuora caught. His hesitation is worrying about how it could come back on him. After all, Figuora can reveal the depth of his involvement.

For now he needs to protect himself, especially since it's not clear what the captain actually knows or what evidence he has on him. Telling them the other location will put him in deeper.

"No, captain, I don't know anything about another location. I only saw him at the rectory."

"Charles, that's hard to believe. This operation appears to be active for the past four years. You must know something."

"I don't know about it being active that long. My information came to me from Skunk. Figuora is tightlipped."

"We need to save the girl, Upton. If anything happens to her and you know something, it will come back on you. You realize that, don't you?"

"I know what happened here with Figuora wasn't handled well by me or Youngblood, for that matter, but we did come to you. If I had a location, I would tell you, cap."

Youngblood's worst fears confirmed, he watches this failed interrogation. He stands listening behind the glass, and he knows the captain is not going to make any further progress. He hopes Urie has better luck. He knows he will.

Urie is walking around their prisoner, sizing him up and working to make him uncomfortable with the unknown of what may happen to him.

"What do they call you?"

"I'm called Clarkson in town. Father Clarkson."

"What's the other one's name?"

"Father Payne."

"Does Figuora have another location in town for his operation?"

"I don't know."

"Not a good answer. I'm short on time. Karl, loosen him up."

Karl comes over and works him, works him hard. Urie is determined to get answers. He waves Karl off as Clarkson catches his breath.

"Well, Clarkson, do they have another location?"

"No no. I don't know. I came into town and was only at one location, the rectory. I was at no other location!"

"Again, Karl."

Clarkson yells, "Why would I lie?" But Urie stands steadfast as Karl goes back to work on Clarkson, who gasps for air. Karl's head hits the light hanging over them, sending shadows around the room and back to reveal the prisoner. Karl moves silently and swiftly, moving, hitting, finding different marks on his body. Clarkson's face is swollen and bloody; his head hangs down.

Karl grabs his hair to lift his head. Urie asks again. "Well?"

"I don't know!"

"That's enough for now, Karl. Leave him here. I'll be back."

Urie and Alexander head back to the main house study. Neither one of them believes he knows anything because with Karl's work, he would have given it up. Entering the study, Urie sits behind his desk.

"I'm going to let him think we'll be back to ask him again."

Just then, Urie's phone rings; it's Youngblood. "Urie, I'm in the precinct, and we just finished talking with Upton. He says he doesn't know of any other location. How did you do with the prisoner?"

"The same. His name is Clarkson and his partner is called Payne. That's all I've got right now from him, but I feel pretty confident he doesn't know the other location. I bet Upton does. Why don't you bring him here? I can find out what he knows."

"I would if I could, but it's not possible. Keep you informed." Youngblood hangs up the phone.

30

Everyone at the Acof household has a tough night and no desire to do anything that morning.

Alexander slept in the guest room where Leslie's perfumed scent is present. This is as close as he can be to her right now. He could slay a dragon, run into a burning building for her, yet right now, there is nothing he can do. They did not get the ransom call they were hoping for last night, consuming him in anger with nowhere to channel it. Princess roamed the house last night. Alexander thinks she is looking for Leslie.

Olga's night is spent in her kitchen. She baked all night with Queen by her side. The smells coming from the kitchen fills the house. This is her way to deal. She quietly goes about her work, praying as she goes.

Urie's night is spent in his study, sitting in his chair. He went over to talk with Clarkson one more time during the night, but he did not let Karl touch him. He keeps thinking about how he is going to stop this. His mind is replaying everything leading up to today, looking for something, anything to help. He takes a series of catnaps out of sheer exhaustion.

He has Carl install a trip sensor on the logging trail, and he and Bertoli take turns patrolling the property with King and Duke rotating two hours on and two hours off.

Karl slept in a cot set by the bank of monitors. If anyone comes on the property or trips the sensor, a buzz will signal him no matter which location.

Urie is done replaying how they got here. It's time to stop wasting time. He accepts that it's too late to figure out where they went wrong; it's time to figure out how to go right and find Figuora.

Without a ransom call, Figuora is making them wait, buying himself time, but for what reason? He didn't have that answer, but one thing is for sure, the real trouble starts after they hear from Figuora. It is time to gather together to talk.

Urie uses the intercom, asking the cook to prepare breakfast for 9:00 a.m. He tells him to let everyone know they are to meet in the kitchen, taking no excuses.

Everyone comes as directed with the last person to arrive being Sergeant Youngblood.

"Good morning everyone. I want you all to rest here at the main house, sleep, read, watch television, do whatever you want, but get some rest. The only person on duty this morning will be you, Bertoli, at the carriage house." Urie can tell by their faces that they think he is losing it.

Youngblood is the first to speak. "What will that accomplish?"

"I'm positive Leslie is just fine. Yes, she's in hostile hands, but right now she is fine. We will hear from Figuora soon. He is tying up loose ends. Most likely, shipping the last bits of that large shipment that Clarkson told us about. Once he has his money, he'll contact us. There will be nothing to keep him here once that happens except to make certain people pay like Leslie and Alexander. Possibly Upton."

"So you believe there will be a ransom for Leslie? And if there is one and you pay it, do you think it will ensure her safety?"

"I believe there will be a ransom request; and no, if we give the money to him, Leslie is dead. This I'm sure about. He'll also want one or more of us, especially you, Alexander."

"So what's your plan? I'm guessing you have one. Am I right, Urie?"

"Figuora is going to ask for ransom money since he has what we want. He will ask for one, two, or even five million dollars."

"How can you be so sure?"

"We intercepted $380,000; they responded by sending two hit men, and now they have to leave this lucrative location. They will want us to pay. Figuora is hung up on revenge, and I think it makes him predictable."

"So Figuora wants revenge on everyone here besides Leslie."

"Correct. Figuora will try to weaken our personnel somehow, someway. Split us up, use the other hit man to get to us, and he will come and come here; so we need to take him alive. If we're going to save Leslie, we need him to tell us her location."

Everyone is quiet as they think through what Urie shared. It's hard for anyone to eat breakfast, but they know what Urie is asking of them is the right thing to do no matter how hard it is. Urie breaks the silence once again.

"This is all we have unless the police come up with something or come across Figuora, but we can't count on them. We have to be prepared, we have to rest and get strong, we will be making plans on the fly. I will have a better plan with your help, so please, rest up and get prepared."

At the warehouse, Figuora and Payne go over what he needs. He wants all the drug money in the van before they deal with the Acofs. Figuora doesn't have this portion of his plan formulated as he is too focused on the money. He wants the women kept healthy until he determines their fate.

"Payne, it's time for the women to use the restroom. Give them water and something to eat."

"I'll take care of it, Figuora."

Leslie hears the footsteps approaching, the padlock being removed, and the door opens. In walks Father Payne.

"Wake up, ladies. Who needs to use the restroom first?"

Payne doesn't wait for a response and approaches Mrs. O'Brien to remove the bungee cords and duct tape, escorting her out of the room. Leslie slowly rolls herself over to the door. Looking up the hall, she spots screwdrivers lying between several boxes. From her vantage point, it's hard to determine if any are Philips head, and based on her scouting out the room last night, she needs a Phillips head to remove a board from the window. This was their way out.

She hears Father Payne's voice, and she slowly pushes her way back to where she sat before he left the room. Payne walks Mrs. O'Brien back into the room to her chair and secures her once again, bungee rope tied around her waist and legs and then taped. He leaves her arms free.

"Your turn, Leslie."

Payne leads her to the bathroom. Passing the tools, she casually glances down and sees two Phillips head screwdrivers. Now all she needs is to find a way to pick one of them up.

Leslie is back in the chair, and Payne is securing her similar to the way he secured Mrs. O'Brien. He hands them both a bottle of water and a tuna fish sandwich, giving them five minutes to finish. Payne stands by the door, counting off the minutes. Once five minutes is reached, he collects whatever food and water is left, securing each woman's hands together with duct tape. Satisfied with the completion of this deed, he leaves, locking the door.

The day is uneventful for the two ladies. Leslie can see, by the loss of light, that the end of another day approaches.

It's near 7:00 p.m., and Figuora is certain that by this time tomorrow, he will correct all the problems and retrieve all the drug money. It will take some extra time to deal with Alexander and his family.

"Payne, let's give the girls another break, and this time bring Leslie up here to me."

Payne is restless and tired of taking care of the ladies. "How soon before I can go to the mansion and have some fun?"

"Soon, Payne. You will have the privilege of eliminating Alexander's parents. Let him live with that! It will be fun to thin the herd. Now bring Leslie to me."

Payne goes through the restroom and feeding ritual again. The only difference is bringing Leslie to the front office and Figuora.

"Leslie, please sit. You're going to be fine. We'll call your boyfriend now and make the arrangements for your release along with Mrs. O'Brien. I'm warning you, do not talk while I'm on the telephone until I ask you to and then no secret code words or clues. Nothing like that at all, or your future and that of Mrs. O'Brien will change drastically. Understand?"

Leslie nods her acknowledgement. Retrieving the Phillips head screwdriver is her primary thought as Figuora picks up the telephone to call Alexander.

"Hello."

"Alexander Acof, this is Father Figuora."

"Is Leslie all right?"

"First things first, Alexander. I need to speak with both you and your father. Can you do this?"

"Yes, I'll put you on speaker phone. Give me a minute."

"Before you do, who else is there with you? Sergeant Youngblood?"

"No, just me and my dad. Youngblood is out looking for Leslie and you."

"Okay, put me on speakerphone."

"Father Figuora, this is Urie Acof."

"Urie, let's skip the formalities. Just call me Frank. Okay, here's what I want. Two million in cash plus the return of the $380,000 your son saw clear to take. Once I have both, you get Leslie and Mrs. O'Brien."

"I will get the money together, Frank. Let me talk with Leslie."

"Easy now, Urie. We need to discuss how the exchange will happen. I want the big bodyguard of yours to drive Alexander to Main Street at 8:00 p.m. tomorrow night by the church. Alexander needs to be standing in the rear of his truck with the money in a bag he can toss. I will have one of my men coming from the opposite direction. He'll flash his high beams, giving you the signal to have your son toss the bag of money into the back of his pickup truck. Understand?"

"Yes. Can I talk to Leslie now?"

"I'm not done, Urie. At the same time, I want your other bodyguard standing in front of the Greyhound bus terminal. I'll have someone there to confirm he's actually there. Oh, and one last thing, you and your wife will remain home. I'll call to confirm you're both there. Everyone needs to be in the locations I've indicated in order for this to go without a hitch. Understand?"

"Understood."

"It's only after I count the money to confirm it's all there that I'll have Leslie and Mrs. O'Brien delivered. Have both bodyguards and Alexander at the Greyhound terminal."

"These terms are unacceptable, Frank. You're getting everything, and we have nothing. Once the money is dropped off, we want the women."

"Can't do it, Urie, but I will let you talk to the women at the same time the money is being dropped off. That's the best I can do. Now, here is Leslie."

"Alexander?"

"Leslie, are you all right?"

"I'm fine, but I wish I had the royalty with me."

Figuora pulls the telephone receiver away from Leslie. "Happy? Now, I'll call you tomorrow during the exchange." He hangs up the phone.

Figuora eyes Leslie, wondering what she meant by the royalty comment. He decides it's not important and has Payne take her back to the room. Payne grabs Leslie by her hair and pulls her out of the door, pushing her toward the lock-up room. She exaggerates his push by falling into the boxes in the hallway, grabs the screwdriver, and shoves it inside her blouse.

Back in the room, Payne tapes Leslie to the chair and uses extra tape around her wrists. She has no flexibility this time. He doesn't tape her mouth. He shoves her toward the corner roughly, and she hits her head on the wall, practically knocking her out. Mrs. O'Brien can only watch quietly. She holds on to her water bottle as Payne makes his way out of the room and locks the door.

Urie is contemplating their new plan of action now that Figuora has them split up, just as he anticipated. He asks his son, "Alexander, what did Leslie mean by royalty?"

"I'm not sure. She's referring to the day we hiked to the lake. We had the dogs with us, and she said it was like she is royalty having them with us."

"We have some time to prepare. Everyone, please take my advice and relax, sleep, read, whatever will restore you and make you strong. I need a few hours to figure out what we're going to do now that we know Figuora's demands. So leave me alone. Please close the door behind you."

31

Urie emerges from his study several hours later. Everyone is in the dining room, even Youngblood.

"Here's what we're going to do. Sergeant, I'm not sending my son to make that exchange. I need you to do it, you're both the same size, and with a baseball cap at night, anyone would be hard-pressed to tell the difference. Alexander, you will be here with me. I'm also keeping Karl. So Youngblood, we need a cop of similar size to use in Karl's place."

"We have someone I can use. What else?"

"The way I figure it, that other hit man, Payne, will be coming here while everyone else is off following Figuora's plan. He wants to eliminate me and my wife, so he can hurt Alexander. It's his payback. If we're going to find Leslie, we need to get Payne alive. He'll know the location."

"Urie, the police can do this."

"No, we can't take that chance. If there's a screwup, we won't have time to get it right again. The fewer the people who know our plan, the better. Once we have Payne, getting the information from him needs

159

to be handled in a certain way."

Youngblood can't believe he is actually going along with this. "I must be nuts, Urie, but I'll do it your way. The captain will need to know what we're doing in order for me and another cop to be involved."

Urie walks over to Carl, putting both hands on his shoulders, squeezing. "Carl, I'm sorry. You will still have to go to the Greyhound bus terminal. You may be a sitting duck."

"I have no problem with this, sir. I only have one request, and that is to let me get the information from Payne once he's captured. Karl always has all the fun."

Urie pats his back, smiling. This man is so loyal. "Carl, you are my man. I don't believe you to be a target, but it's better to go in thinking you are. Figuora wants minimum staff here to make it easier for Payne to get in. I want you to wear a flak jacket to be prepared, just in case."

"Yes sir."

"As for the rest of us, I'm still formulating the part each of us will play. So Olga, Alexander, Karl, and Bertoli, we'll talk later."

Alexander is so proud of his dad. He's organized, detailed, and a good judge of people. With all the things in their favor, Alexander can't understand why he has such a bad feeling in his stomach.

"Karl, while I'm gone, I need you to get a duffel bag big enough to hold two million dollars and fill it with newspapers. I need you to pull out four pairs of night vision glasses, four chairs placed in the attic, and make sure all the windows are clean. We need five headsets so we can communicate. Everyone is to select their weapon of choice. Make sure it's something you're comfortable with and, Karl, pull one Taser. While you're doing that, I am going with Sergeant Youngblood to talk with his captain. Alexander, you follow us in the Hummer. When I return, we'll get back together to go through our plan. Are we all good?"

Urie looks around the room, and everyone is nodding their agreement. He keeps his eyes on Sergeant Youngblood a few seconds longer than anyone else. He is surprised he does not hear any pushback from him.

"Well, that's it then. Let's go, sergeant. Alexander, meet us out front."

"Sergeant, I must tell you, I appreciate the trust you're placing in me and my family."

"I have done things I never thought I would since I met your family."

"I know, Harold. You must feel a little out of character, but these criminals are not playing by the rules. To get Leslie back, we don't need out hands tied."

"One question, is Clarkson still with us?"

"Yes, he is. A little bruised but still with us."

"So at the end of all this, do you think we'll have Payne, Clarkson, and Figuora in our custody?"

"Yes, I most certainly do, probably more. One thing I almost forgot, here is a cell phone for you. It's a burner. It's for me to get in touch with you. No one has the number except me. I entered my number in there for you too. Youngblood, I need you to stretch out the money drop. Do something to slow it down like being in the wrong lane, dropping the duffle bag, something like that. This will give us the time we need to get Figuora."

"Where do you think he'll be?"

"Figuora is going out of his way to ensure we have minimal personnel at the mansion, and he's strategically locating his hit man and a few others. He's going to be at the location where he's holding the women. That's why it's so important we get Payne first."

Figuora and Payne feel satisfied that everything is in place to their advantage.

"Payne, when you're finished with the work at the mansion, call me, and I'll have you picked up. We will meet at a location I have in mind. Take the two million plus the drug money and get out of town."

"Where do we go from there?"

"This towns going to be hot. Everything of importance will be with us in the van, and we'll return to Mexico and Carlos. Have no fear."

"What about the women?"

"Once you call me to tell me you're done, I'll take care of them."

Back at the precinct, Youngblood is with Urie, speaking to the captain, giving him his spin on what's needed and why. While he tells his tale, Urie sits quietly so not to sabotage the apparent progress he is making.

"Mr. Acof, I have to agree with Sergeant Youngblood. We need to make the drop and use two of our policemen, one behind the wheel and Youngblood in the back of the pickup. This is not a job for civilians, and our personnel are trained for this type of situation."

"I feel much better already, captain. Thank you."

"Would you like extra protection at your home, Mr. Acof?"

"No, captain, not at the house; but if you could leave the patrol car at the end of our driveway and add another about one mile south of the house at the intersection, that would be good. If someone is going to come, they most likely will approach from that direction."

"You can count on us to do that. We'll have them there. You and your son should go to your home now. We'll take it from here. We'll be in touch."

"Sergeant Youngblood, come back with us to get the duffle bag of money. It should be ready for you, and Alexander will give you his work jacket and baseball cap. Thanks again, captain. Is it okay if we leave now?"

"Yes, let's get those things in the works. Youngblood, take charge of the money, get the clothes, and let's put a tracking device inside the bag to be on the safe side."

Outside the precinct, clear of anyone's earshot, Youngblood asks Urie, "Why the patrol car only to the south of your location?"

"I'm thinking Payne will try to enter the property on the logging road, which is how he escaped the last time. If a patrol car is to the south, this will force him to use the north access."

"What does that gain you?"

"The carriage house is in that direction, and I want him approaching that way if possible. If not, we'll have to quickly make other plans."

"Understood, Urie."

32

Alexander follows his father and Youngblood back to the property. He has a new appreciation for this town. The town he loves, filled with hard-working people doing their daily deeds, each making life better for them all—school bus drivers, the cleaners, the bank, plumbing and supply—all kinds of people with families and children, working side by side. They did not need Figuora. His operation tears a town apart. Drugs are a curse, not allowing good people to lead a normal life any longer. The drugs stop any resemblance to normal life like the Norman Rockwell painting this area should be. Figuora needs to be stopped.

It is late by the time he parks the Hummer, sets Youngblood up with his clothes, and says good night.

Once back at the house, Alexander asks his father, "Do you think we can get Leslie back safely?"

"Yes, Alexander, I do. Figuora is blinded by hubris. He's dealt with the homeless who have no confidence in themselves. He makes them drug dependent so they will do almost anything for their next high. He's forgotten how normal people live, think, and he's underestimating us. That is why we will get Payne and find the women. We will get them all."

Urie asks Carl to have everyone up at the main house kitchen by 7:00 a.m. the next morning. He says good night to Alexander and heads to his study to finish up a few details. When he enters the room, his wife Olga is sitting by his desk waiting for him.

"How did everything go?"

"Youngblood gained the support of his captain."

"Urie, you're not planning on staying up all night again are you?"

"I have to work out a few more details, honey."

"You know I love you and have complete faith in your ability to work this thing out. You have always been such a good man protecting us. What if this man Payne doesn't come here?"

"I'm afraid there is a bigger chance that Leslie will be killed. Unless the police can somehow stumble onto Figuora or Payne and extract Leslie's location from them."

"Can we search for her?"

"I've thought about that. We feel confident they have gone north of the rectory, but that's still a lot of town to consider. If we did come across Leslie, it would be by luck. Figuora has an army of homeless people which he feeds food and drugs. They are his loyal followers who would not break the code. Our only hope is to get Payne."

Olga is as satisfied as she can be under the circumstances. She wishes there is something else they could do. "You must be hungry."

"No thanks, honey, but I could use some of your fine coffee."

Over at the warehouse, Mrs. O'Brien imitates what Leslie did earlier and digs her heels into the floor, pushing her chair over to where Leslie is passed out. Her hands, still free from dinner, she touches Leslie's wrist to get a pulse. She is convinced Payne has an issue with her by what he's done so far, and the way he's tied her to the chair confirms it. Even Houdini would be unable to escape. She thinks about waking Leslie up but decides to let her sleep. Before she pushes herself back to the other side of the room, she sees the screwdriver sticking out of Leslie's shirt. Mrs. O'Brien gently removes the screwdriver, thinking how Leslie must have this for a reason, and she better hide it.

6:00 a.m. arrives, and Urie's wristwatch alarm tells him. He took several catnaps during the night, but his body is not fully rested. He moves into a hot shower, hoping to feel better, and prepares to join everyone at seven in the dining room.

Sergeant Youngblood is the only person missing. Urie thinks perhaps he fears this morning's discussion contains details he's better off not knowing. Urie smiles. He's a good man with a strong "go by the book" belief, he thinks. He needs to spend a little more time around them. Urie is sure he can help him make an adjustment.

"How is everyone?"

"Ready," everyone answers in unison.

"Good. Since the drop is at eight this evening, we all need to be in place by 6:00 p.m. Karl, are we all set with the things you were working on yesterday?"

"Yes, sir, all set and ready."

"Good. Then let me start with you and Bertoli. I want both of you over in the carriage house. Bert, you monitor the security screens for us, and Karl, you need to be armed and ready, waiting for Payne. We'll meet over there in a few hours to go into more detail. Carl, make sure you have on the flak jacket, and I want you to carry a handgun. Once you hear the drop is made, get back here as fast as you can. You will know what's going on from the police wire we're going to give you. Keep your vehicle close."

"Yes, sir."

"Olga, I want all the lights on downstairs on the first floor. At six, I want you at the west attic window with night vision goggles on. I don't anticipate Payne coming from that direction, but once Payne is spotted, you are to go down to the front door and let Bertoli in then reset the alarm. Proceed upstairs and turn the lights on up there to make it look like we have people getting ready to go to bed. Bertoli, I will let you know when to come over to the house. Use the ATV and leave the garage door open. Olga will let you into the main house through the front door. Once you're in, start turning off the lights on the first floor."

"I can do this."

"Me too Urie."

"You, Alexander, I want your young eyes at the north end of the attic. Once you spot Payne, and Bert has the lights off downstairs, we go down to the first floor."

Over at the warehouse, Payne is about to let the women use the restroom. He is delighted to see Leslie is still out, and his joy is apparent to Mrs. O'Brien. "Umm, she slept good last night, didn't she, Mrs. O?"

"I'm wondering if we can get some blankets for tonight. It gets awfully cold in here."

"Sure, but first let's take you to the restroom."

Payne takes Mrs. O'Brien to the bathroom, returning to tie her down as usual, only securing one wrist this time. He does not see her as a risk. He hands her a bottle of Gatorade and a tuna sandwich. Walking over to Leslie, he cracks open smelling salts and holds it under her nose. She comes to, coughing. "Time to get to the bathroom."

He follows the same routine with Leslie and returns her to her chair, securing her more steadfastly when Figuora sticks his head in the room. "I need her alert, so be gentle with her, Payne."

He continues to tape her in extra tight, but it is clear the pushing of the chair is out of the question. His fun is ruined this morning. He enjoys seeing people suffer. Leaving the room, he padlocks the door and walks away. Inside, Mrs. O'Brien listens to the sound of his retreating footsteps. She digs in her heels and pulls herself over to Leslie who is crying. "Stop that, Leslie. Everything is going to be okay."

Leslie looks at this dirty-faced woman with her messed-up hair. "I've lost the screwdriver I took yesterday. It's gone."

"You didn't lose it. I took it from you last night and hid it in the insulation over there. I didn't want them to find it."

Leslie's smile returns. "You are one in a million."

"Mrs. O'Brien, I have a plan. They won't be back to check on us until later this afternoon, so we need to get busy. Can you push your chair over to that window? Once you get there, you will see a sharp piece of glass on the windowsill. We're going to need that to cut through the tape."

Mrs. O'Brien does as she is asked. Making her way over to the window, she squirms in her chair, stretching the ropes out as far as she can. With one final movement, she gets her fingers up on the windowsill and walks them down to the glass shard. Making sure their firmly in place, she pushes her chair back away from the window, and the glass shard slips into her hand between two fingers. She shows Leslie the piece of glass, holding it up like a trophy.

Mrs. O'Brien slides her chair back to where Leslie is seated and makes fast work of cutting her free. Once she has a free hand, Leslie takes the glass from Mrs. O'Brien and cuts the rest of her bonds then gets to work freeing her. Both women are now standing, and it feels really good.

"Go listen by the door and be quiet."

Leslie retrieves the screwdriver from the insulation, working quickly to remove the bottom board. Looking outside, it is later than she anticipated as the sun is lower in the sky than it would be in the afternoon. She has to hurry. She needs to remove another board to make the opening big enough for them to squeeze through. She begins to work on the next board and realizes the screws are stripped. In an instant, the fear she's been fighting comes back full force, but she pushes it down, remembering what she learned from Alexander.

If a screw is stripped, it most likely happened going in. To get it out, you need to push your screwdriver into the screw head, putting a strong hold on the screwdriver and flattening the palm of your hand at its end. Using your body weight, bounce your palm and twist the screwdriver with each bounce.

Each time she does this, the screw moves out a quarter of a turn, sometimes more. The more it moves out, the easier it gets. Leslie realizes removing one screw is enough, and she rotates the board out of the way.

"Come on, Mrs. O'Brien. It's time to get out of here."

Leslie slides through first followed by Mrs. O'Brien, who comes out head first. It is a good thing she is small enough for Leslie to catch. There is high grass all around the brick buildings to the rear and down across the yard. Leslie spots that beautiful junk pile behind John's pawnshop, and it never looked better.

"This way, Mrs. O'Brien."

They cut across the yard, hop a low fence, and they're on their way to John's fenced-in property. Leslie cannot believe her luck when she spots a hole in this fence big enough for them to squeeze through.

She is grateful the night's beginning to get dark, but it made for slow progress because of all John's treasures. There are machines, cars, crates, and lots of metal. Finally she sees the rear garage door. This is their destination, and the last leg of their approach is out in the open. Before they step out of the shadows, she hears yelling.

"They're outside. They must be in with that junk. Get men over there and find them. Now." This voice is unmistakable; it's Figuora's.

Leslie and Mrs. O'Brien hear them coming; they cannot chance running to the door because they will be out in the open and easily spotted. Leslie recalls there are two piles of lumber reaching about twelve feet high. She places her index finger in front of her lips to signal their need to be silent and grabs Mrs. O'Brien's hand, leading her in that direction. There is a narrow space between the two piles of lumber. Leslie shoves Mrs. O'Brien in first, and she slides right in and out of sight. Leslie is a few steps in when her shirt gets caught wedging her in place. If not for Mrs. O'Brien reaching out to grab her, there's no telling what might have happened. The lumber is up against a part of the fence with a building behind it. They find a small space in the back and quickly huddle together to hide just as the sound of footsteps on gravel can be heard scrambling back and forth. A flashlight shines down between the lumber. They are just out of its beam.

Figuora is there. "If I find them, they're dead." It's Payne. "No, Payne, we still need them or at least Leslie." Their voices are clear, and both women hug each other tightly.

"Payne, they're not here. Let's leave the boys out here because we need to get moving; otherwise, we're going to run out of time."

Over at the carriage house, Urie is going over their plans with Bertoli and Karl.

"Bertoli, when I tell you to come to the main house, leave here, exiting the garage. Take an ATV and drive slowly as if you have all the time in the world. The important thing is to leave the garage door open, and Karl, take this Taser gun. We need him alive."

Urie made sure everyone understands the plan and returns to the main house. Carl is leaving for his location. Tonight is an important night for everyone. There is little time for conversation as everyone concentrates on their role. The lives of Leslie and Mrs. O'Brien and their safety rest on executing their plan. By six o'clock, everyone is in place.

33

Payne is driven to the Acof property by one of Figuora's homeless helpers. They move slowly through the wooded roads, maintaining the posted speed. As they approach the intersection to the south of the property, they spot a police car parked as security. Without slowing down or any hesitation, he orders his driver to continue straight on the road, suggesting they see what lies up ahead. His driver does as instructed. Before too long, they come up to the mansion driveway where he spots the second police car.

"Maintain our speed. Just keep driving." Approaching the northern edge of the Acof property, Payne has to smile. There is no one there. He shakes his head at the poor planning on the part of the Acof family and decides this is the place for him to make his entry. It's probably better than the logging trail, which would surely be watched since that's how they gained their entry the last time and how he escaped. "Pull over and drop me here. Don't go back the same way we came. You'll get a call when you need to come get me."

Payne exits the car and backs up into the darkness of the woods. He watches as the car proceeds up the road, over the hill, and disappears. He waits a few moments. Once he is satisfied there isn't any movement around him, he silently crosses the road. He enters the woods and checks his watch. It's six thirty. He needs to get moving to be in position by seven thirty.

Payne heads east, following the lights from the mansion that glow in the night's sky. He stumbles upon a deer trail and follows it for as long as he can. The rocks and moss make his footing tough and unstable. When he finally crests the hill, he finds himself fifty yards behind the carriage house.

Alexander is scanning the property for Payne's arrival. He's picked up the heat outline of a figure emerging from the woods, using the infrared camera. It will take time before he's able to actually determine who it is. "I have someone at two o'clock behind the carriage house. Right now, whoever it is, is stationary in the cluster of pines."

Urie turns his head in that direction. "I have him." On cue, Olga goes downstairs to the front door. Queen walks with her every step of the way. "Did you hear that, Karl?"

"Yes, sir."

Payne glances down at his watch. It's taken him longer to get here because of the unanticipated change in entering the property. It is now seven ten.

"He is stationary in the same spot."

Urie speaks into his ear communication device, "Bertoli, do your thing."

Bertoli moves down to the basement garage. He gets on an ATV, slipping his Glock into his vest, and opens the garage door. Doing as planned, he moves slowly without a care in the world. He even stops to light a cigarette then continues in the direction of the main house.

Olga is there. She's disengaged the alarm and lets him in. Bertoli waits a few minutes and begins to turn off all the first-floor lights moving room to room. Olga resets the alarm and proceeds upstairs to turn on all the lights.

Payne is delighted to see they're not showing any concern that someone like him could be coming here. He is going to eliminate whoever is in the carriage house first, thinning out the personnel.

"He's on the move."

"He's drawing close to the carriage house and will be there soon. Out of sight, Karl."

"I'm ready." Bertoli reports the first floor lights are off, and Urie lets everyone know he is heading down to the carriage house. Urie, King and Duke head for the first floor. Alexander will join them once Payne is out of his line of sight.

As Payne reaches the garage door, he thinks how well off this family is and how Figuora should have asked for five million dollars. With gun in hand, Payne walks up to the basement door. Seeing no sensor, he opens the door to enter the basement. The lighting is dull and barely illuminates the staircase going up. He reaches the top landing with ease and moves swiftly. Cracking the door open, his eyes take in a security room lined with monitors. There is a figure at the control panel wearing a headset. Payne opens the door wide enough for him to enter, moving in the man's direction. A cup of coffee sits on the table with the steam still rising. Payne is thrilled by how easy this is going to be. He walks silently right up to this man and, looking out the window, takes in the main house with the lights glowing on the second floor.

He's happy to think everyone's getting ready for bed. He moves his gun into position and puts a round into the back of the man's head. Holstering his weapon, he grabs the chair to spin it around so he can see the man's face, curious to know who he got. He is taken aback. "Clarkson, shit." That is all he can say because in the next moment, Karl shoots him with his Taser, knocking him to the ground. "I've got him."

Alexander and Urie are out the door to the ATV in no time, heading over to the carriage house. Olga, Bertoli, Queen, and Princess stay behind. When they enter the carriage house, Karl is securing Payne to a chair. Urie pulls out his burner phone and let's Youngblood know they have Payne, and he needs to stretch out the drop off as long as possible. Karl breaks open a popper under Payne's nose; he comes to, sees Urie, and smiles.

"You're too late old man, the women are dead."

Karl looks at Urie. "We cannot wait for Carl. I need to take care of this now." Urie nods in agreement. Karl works over Payne, but so far, the information they need is not forthcoming. Payne just keeps saying things to taunt them. Things like "Both women are dead."

Alexander shoots Payne in the kneecap. "There are plenty of places I can do that and still keep you alive. No problem."

At the warehouse, Figuora exits the back door and yells to his men, "Any sight of them?"

"No, they're not out here."

"Okay, get inside." Leslie and Mrs. O'Brien stay huddled together for warmth even though they hear Figuora's instructions.

Frank is back inside the warehouse where he tells everyone to stay put. He warns them to get ready for once Payne and the team picking up the ransom return; they'll need to move. He gets into the van and drives out of the warehouse. He knows the drop is doomed without Leslie's voice, and if she's managed to contact the police somehow, this place will be crawling with them in no time. Without any doubt, he decides it's best for him to leave.

Leslie and Mrs. O'Brien shiver in the night air. Even though their hiding place is small and they huddle, it's still cold. Leslie hears the crackle of the gravel and steps approaching. They hold their breath. There's a voice, a quiet voice, "Leslie?" It's John.

"John?"

"Yes. I'm alone. Hurry before they come back." The two women wiggle their way to the opening, and John leads them to the small access door housed in the garage door. Once inside, Leslie hugs and kisses John.

"I need to use a phone."

34

Alexander hears his cell phone ring and reads the display. He looks at Urie and tells him it's John. "Yes?"

"It's me, Leslie."

"Are you with my friend?"

"Yes, we both are and we're safe. We were being held in the building next to John's pawnshop."

"Stay put. I'll be there as soon as I can. You're safe now."

Alexander shoots Payne in the other knee. Looking at his dad, he lets him know, "Leslie is safe. She was being held in an old abandoned warehouse."

Karl shakes his head at the condition Payne is in. "My brother is going to be pissed."

Urie once again uses his burner phone to call Youngblood. His goal is to let him know Leslie and Mrs. O'Brien are safe and where they were being held but never has the opportunity. Harold is in the back of the pick-up, getting ready to make the transfer. He never answers Urie's call. He can see the other truck approaching.

Once the trucks are next to each other, he makes his move. Instead of tossing the duffle bag over, he launches himself into the bed of the other truck, punches out the back window, and shoves his gun into the driver's head.

"Pull over."

Carl speeds toward the mansion. He passes both police cars so fast they follow him. He pulls up to the carriage house gate, unlocks it, and runs for the basement. Carl looks down at Payne and his condition. "You said he was mine."

Urie walks over to hug him. "I know. It's not what we planned. I owe you one."

Leslie hangs up the phone. She's listening to Mrs. O'Brien and John talk about his kitchen. She smiles. After all they went through, the conversation about the kitchen is funny. "Yes, these are Wolf stoves."

"I'd love to try my hand at cooking here sometime."

"Sure, Mrs. O, whenever you like." Sitting at the table, Leslie is amused by Mrs. O'Brien who is like a kid in candy land.

"Are you hungry, dear? We can whip up something for you."

"I'd really like some water and a place to freshen up."

John disappears into the warehouse and returns with clean clothes. "These should fit you. Follow me. I think a shower is just what you need."

He takes her to the bathroom. It is complete with a rainfall showerhead and a huge claw foot tub. "Take a bath if you prefer. There's bubble bath, linens, and shampoo in the closet."

Leslie loves the bathroom. She is in awe of how beautiful his living areas are. His bathroom is on the same scale as his kitchen, gorgeous. The business he's in conflicts with his clean, orderly living quarters. She grabs the bubble bath and immerses herself in a hot bath. Her chill is gone, and she feels clean again.

Alexander couldn't leave the property with more police arriving. He learns they are also being dispatched to the warehouse and the pawnshop. He's anxious to see Leslie, but he and Urie realize it will look better for Sergeant Youngblood if they stay while the police finish their work. They are grateful to him for all his help. It's the least they can do.

Youngblood calls them about ten p.m., saying he's on his way with Leslie.

Alexander sits on the front steps, waiting. When Youngblood's cruiser pulls up to the fountain, he gets pushed to the side by Mr. and Mrs. Turner as they rush past him to hug their daughter. Leslie looks at him over their shoulders. This is very surreal and borderline hysterical.

Alexander waits a few minutes then walks over and pulls her free, picks her up, and kisses her. Mr. and Mrs. Turner do not object to this man being with their daughter, especially with this house on over two hundred acres. That means money.

Urie asks everyone to join him in the living room. The air is filled with static energy, and everyone is talking at once even Karl and Carl. Leslie listens to some of the things her mother is saying to her dad, words like "Ethan Allen" and "tastefully done."

Urie grabs Youngblood to the side. "What about Figuora?"

"I'm afraid he's disappeared."

"How many people are involved?"

"We arrested over twenty-six people, plus there is Clarkson and Payne. By the way, how did Payne get shot?"

"He tried to escape."

"I'm sure he did."

Urie asks for everyone's attention. "I invite all of you to stay tonight. We have more than enough room, and tomorrow, we'll take everyone out for brunch." Leslie's mom and dad are in agreement.

Leslie's mom can't help herself. "Where will you take us, Urie?"

"To my friend's home. His name is John."

Mrs. O'Brien and Leslie look at each other and laugh. It's a private joke only the inside family understands.

ABOUT THE AUTHOR

June Gilbert has been given a second chance in life to reinvent herself. Her first published work, Deception, is filled with rich characters driven by their work ethic, social values, and motivation. Her characters aren't afraid to influence the things they can influence. Even when their actions flirt with danger.

Like a travel agent, this author takes you on a journey of intrigue, mystery and manipulation with several unexpected twists and turns until you arrive at a predetermined destination.

June lives a life of love with her husband and two dogs. In the Fall and Winter she assembles jigsaw puzzles, cooks, and collects the current years Macy's Day Parade snow globe while in Spring and Summer she loves to read, garden, and spend time outside.

June's past carrier afforded her the opportunity to creatively write under many different circumstances. She is most proud of creating learning opportunities and writing for leadership. She looks forward to applying her skills in her new endeavor of writing fiction.

CPSIA information can be obtained at www.ICGtesting.com
Printed in the USA
BVOW02*0404140415

394727BV00001BA/1/P